DARK

Founded in 1948, Cambridge Writers has expanded over the past 76 years to provide writing meetings, workshops, literary talks and shared writing spaces for local writers. Every year, a short story competition is held for its members. This collection of short stories, *Darkness*, is the group's eighth anthology, and presents a tremendous selection of members' interpretations of the theme and showcases the exceptional talent of the Cambridge Writers group.

Other titles from Cambridge Writers:

SECRETS AND LIES:
Cambridge Writers Short Story Competition 2023

COINCIDENCE:
Cambridge Writers Short Story Competition 2022

VISITORS:
Cambridge Writers Short Story Competition 2021

MOUNTAIN:
Cambridge Writers Short Story Competition 2020

REVENGE:
Cambridge Writers Short Story Competition 2019

FREEDOM:
Cambridge Writers Short Story Competition 2018

Compilation of Cambridge Writers Short Story
Competition Winners 2013-2017

DARKNESS

Cambridge Writers
Annual Short Story Competition 2024
anthology

Foreword by Chris Priestley
Introduction by Harry Goode
Edited by Kathy English, Harry Goode
& Hannah Hooton

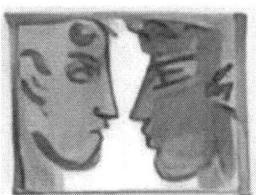

Cambridge Writers

Cover design: Mohammed Sedik Bendaoud © 2024

www.cambridgewriters.org

Contents

Foreword

Chris Priestley

The way we respond to a story is such a personal thing and dependent on so many different factors. We can read a story that did nothing for us twenty years earlier and be blown away. As writers we all just do the best we can and hope it works for the reader.

I find the whole process of ranking stories problematic, I have to say. I think I am dubious about how two different works of art can be compared in that way. I always get a bit twitchy when there is talk of 'best' books, 'best' song or 'best' films. 'Best' in what way? Is *Wuthering Heights* 'better' than *The Talented Mr Ripley*? Is *Taxi Driver* 'better' than *Some Like it Hot*?

I think I have tried as much as I can to judge them as a reader, as much as a writer. My first pass on the stories (I read each of them at least three times) was simply to see if the story grabbed me. Then it was about looking at why and how. I think the standard was really high right across the board. There were stories I felt were a tweak or two away from being spot on. Those edits and tweaks may be tiny but their effect can be – and often are – crucial. Some writers take to Twitter to moan about editing. They love the writing bit, they say. But they aren't two different things. When writers brag about how many words they've written that day I want to ask how many they've lost. Because a good day's writing can often mean you end up with less words than you started with.

I think endings are hugely important in a short story. Not necessarily in the sense of having a twist or some kind of startling reveal, but the reader should have that sense that they have experienced the end – even if that end is ambiguous, if that makes sense. I think all the stories I have chosen had the beginning-middle-end-ness that we all look for as readers but sometimes forget to deliver as writers.

Thank you again for asking me to read these stories. I had no idea what to expect. It was fascinating to see the range of story-making, the scope of the ideas and the different voices. I was really impressed. And I'm not easily impressed. As I said at the start, I'm not an expert, only a fellow writer, but I think you seem to be getting along fine without any advice from me, so I'm going to shut up.

Good luck with all your future writing. I hope I get to read some of it.

Commended (in no particular order)
'A Sunday Afternoon in the Garden'
I liked the gentle, bucolic descriptions of the garden

contrasting with the grimness of the plot. It was very nicely paced, I thought. This was maybe an extra plot point or a twist away from getting into the placings.

'Gotcha!'
This had a Saki-esque quality to it, I thought. And that can never be a bad thing. A very nice atmosphere throughout. Each time I read it, I was intrigued. There was an air of mystery to it.

'The Rookery'
Lovely sense of place here with a really intriguing atmosphere. It had a nice shape to it, with strong characters and dialogue. There was a succession of really memorable moments. So much going on here.

Third Place
'The Coming of Cholera'
This had the feel of a South American magic realist story (or that may be the slight echo of Marquez's *Love in the Time of Cholera* in the title). It had a lovely timeless fable-like quality about it. I felt like this was a very confident piece of writing, particularly that soft ending which seemed perfect for a story of this kind.

Second Place
'The Bone Cleaners'
There was a confidence to this story, I thought. The characters and dialogue felt real. It is a strange story but the level of detail made it feel convincing. I was involved in the plot and I felt like I was in the hands of someone who had a firm grip on proceedings.

First Place

'Twin Lambs'

I liked everything about this: the convincing sense of place and characters, the bold brevity of it, the deft time shift and the emotional charge of the ending. I think it's one thing to be clever – and this story is very clever – and another to be emotionally engaging. To be both is quite something.

Chris Priestley
March, 2024

Introduction

Harry Goode

'Lighten our darkness, we beseech thee, O Lord.' Thus, the Third Collect in the service of evening prayer. I suppose it is suggesting that we sleep with a spiritual night-light.

As usual, the theme for our annual short story competition is chosen by members who attend the Annual General Meeting. In 2023, they chose 'The Dark'.

Darkness is not always seen as a time of terrors. Simon and Garfunkel in *The Sound of Silence*, sing *'Hello darkness, my old friend / I've come to talk with you again.'* A similar sentiment is found in Christophe Barrantier's excellent (albeit somewhat sentimental) film *Les Choristes*. The choir sings Jean-Philippe Rameau's *Hymne à la Nuit* with the line *'le calme enchantement de ton mystère'*

There are bleaker visions of darkness. In his poem *East Coker*, T S Eliot has a jeremiad about the fact that we all go into the dark, even *'eminent men of letters'* – so be warned! He then continues, *'I said to my soul, be still, and let the darkness come upon you/ Which shall be the darkness of God.'* This is neither Simon and Garfunkel's *'old friend'*, nor

Rameau's *'calme enchantement'*. Whether or not you believe in God, the idea that profounder truths may lie in darkness, is an intriguing one.

With every competition we hold, our members can be relied upon to interpret the theme in radically different ways. This time, it was no different. The winners and those who received commendations are to be congratulated, but the richness of this collection is due to all those who took part.

I would like to thank Chris Priestley who acted as our judge and Siobhán Carew who was our Competition Secretary. Hannah Hooton, our Publicity Officer, has put together the stories for publication and Kathy English, our Membership Secretary, has proofread everything.

Harry Goode, Chair
August, 2024

A Bitter-Sweet Dream

Christine Hawkes

He put his hand to the back of the drawer, searching under his usual ties for an old one; feeling a small, cold object, he withdrew it and stared at the perfect, heart shaped pebble. Dan Marshall shook himself. You fool. You silly, old fool. He thought of the person who'd been gathering shells and pebbles on Brighton Beach. Its sandy colour reminded him of her gently tanned skin, how many years ago? The sky was blue, the sea turquoise... and... he'd discovered the stone in his jacket pocket, later that night.

'Are you ready Dan? Your taxi's due and I'm off to Mum's soon. I'll get along later if she's okay. Her twilight carer said she'd "just slipped".' His wife was calling from the hall.

'Just putting a tie on, love. Do try and come, Anne; we'll be there till 11... and... you'll be missed.' His mother-in-law, living nearby had become obsessed, in her dotage, with Christian Science; now, she wouldn't even have her temperature taken, never mind see a doctor or take Vitamin D. Dan's big 'leaving do' at the Greenford Working Men's Club had been arranged for weeks. He

1

found the tie, a pale pink wool one he'd worn when he thought they were trendy. No sneakers tonight, sensible brown, leather brogues. He gave a quick glance in the triple mirror, seeing his greying head too many times and shook it; at least, no one could call him Ginger these days, or trendy, though Robert Redford had once boosted the appeal of sandy hair. He'd worn it long and his mother told him he'd be mistaken for a lass if he didn't tie it up.

Dan looked up at the indigo autumn sky from the taxi window and murmured to himself, 'The moon was a ghostly galleon, tossed upon cloudy seas.' He remembered it from being ten, but what was the poem? Anne would know, she was a primary school teacher. Ahead, from the club were brighter lights to greet him. Red, yellow, green, and blue balloons were dancing, out of time, in a gentle breeze from the rusting railing beside the lacquered door. He took a deep breath and strode inside, inhaling the smell of stale beer and smoke. Just like the club his commercial traveller father went to in Manchester, years ago. Loud voices, laughter and music from a swing band welcomed him. Dan's musical tastes hadn't changed much since his twenties.

'Here he is…!' The shout was accompanied by "Hail, the conquering hero comes…" from the musicians, more used to playing Glen Miller than hammering Handel. Small tables and chairs were at the room's perimeter, well-filled buffet tables before the stage; behind the band, huge golden letters spelt a 'Happy retirement to Dan', who was head of the art department. The bar in a side room was open to accommodate those whose tastes were more inclined to beer than Burgundy or Prosecco. The billiard table was already in use by the regular inhabitants of the club and Dan often made his way to join them, but not tonight.

'Come and sit here, Sir!' from a group of his students in the large room.

'Cor, what a tie, Sir!'

'Dan! There's a special place for you. Over there! Where's Anne?' Yes, Darby and Joan were how the couple were regarded. He didn't think they'd ever been Romeo and Juliet, more firm friendship, and mutual regard, than passion.

As Dan moved on, he was surprised how many names he remembered, despite his sixty-five years.

'Still wearing the gaudy tie, I see. What are you going to do now?' from Mavis in the Textiles department, who already sat at his table. 'Grow cabbages?' Textiles had evolved from Domestic Science: now the students knitted teapots, rather than learn to brew the perfect pot of tea.

Dan smiled patiently and joined her. Oh Mavis… 'Well, no. Hemlock, I think… we tried carrots and got carrot fly, potatoes, then blight. Anne thinks we'll be constantly in Europe when *she* stops, but…' What the hell was he going to do with all that time? Anne would be trapped by her mother's needs, never mind Europe.

'Oh, you must have retirement plans. I have plans, and I'm not going for three years!' bellowed Henry across the table, nearly spilling his pint as he smacked the table for emphasis. 'Aren't you going back to Manchester? I know you came down here to go to art school and you met Anne, but why else did you keep those flat vowels?'

'Only going back to The Lowry Gallery, and a newish one, The Whitworth, on Oxford Road – an interesting building, apparently. No plans, Henry. Anne and I agreed we'd have no plans; just be spontaneous.' A wry grin accompanied his seemingly jocular remark. He was tired of rising to the accent bait yet wouldn't say that after two miscarriages and a hysterectomy, any planning felt tempting fate.

Looking towards the heavy oak door, he saw more arrivals; familiar faces scanned the room till they caught sight of him and waved or yelled; then when seeing old friends and other colleagues, yelled, and waved at them. And still the band played – at times so loudly it was hard to hear even one's neighbour. Dan looked surreptitiously at a small card, reminding him who to thank. The music stopped and the head of Upper School stood on the stage, smiling, and touching her dried lips with a red-nailed finger. She beckoned to Dan, who threaded his way forward, ducking a thumping on the back. He caught sight of someone he hadn't seen for years, and his heart lurched. She had her arm round the shoulders of an adolescent, red-haired girl and smiled as he passed them.

Dan gave an amusing and emotional speech, not forgetting to thank those who had made such a wonderful evening possible and shook hands with the band leader. Then there were presents, more speeches, more laughter, more cheers. Flowers for Anne, white roses, purple and white freesia with eucalyptus, and regrets for her absence. The most precious gift of all: a small, signed limited edition print of a Miro painting, which Dan had coveted. Anne must have told somebody. He looked round the hall in case his wife had suddenly arrived. Then a voice came from the back. 'Now it's time for True or False!' to be met by laughter and stamping. Dan hoped he would be excused the possible embarrassment of that popular inclusion at farewell gatherings. He made his way back to his seat and speculated about the woman and girl. If he and Anne had been able to have a family, might they have had a red-haired daughter?

Everyone was quiet, looking expectantly at Dan as he came out of his revery.

'Come on Dan! True or False?'

'Sorry. What was the question?'

'Who got drunk when we had the trip to Brighton Pavilion in 1995?'

A roar went up and shrieks of laughter spread through a small group of old pupils near the stage. A woman, probably in her forties, stepped forward and defended him. 'I was the drunk one and Mr. Marshall protected me.' More laughter and banter and the questions moved from Dan's possible mishaps to other staff, their gaffes in school and on study trips.

He appeared to be involved in the festivities, but Dan was thinking about the trip to Brighton. Diana Wood, supporting him here tonight: the brightest and best of his students in that year and given a third year in the sixth form, after her father died. He was an architect, Dan remembered. He had felt protective, understanding her pain from his own losses, and so took a fatherly interest although he was much younger than her parent had been. The band started to play Miller's 'A String of Pearls' and the lights were lowered; couples moved away from the tables and empty plates to glide under an old glitter ball, which provided a touch of nostalgia and the party atmosphere.

Diana Wood was standing beside him, her blue silk shirt intensifying her blue eyes. 'Dancing, Sir?' Dan hesitated and then took the proffered hand and led her to the dancing shadows on the floor. Looks of approval greeted him as they glided towards the rotating stars of light, thrown by beams from the silver globe.

'Where's your... daughter?' he ventured.

'Oh, her father came to take her home. She just wanted to see who I'd been to school with. We, Jack and I, came to see my parents for the weekend. And you are still *here*!'

'Jack? Is he tall, red-haired? I saw someone come in I didn't recognise.'

She smiled. 'I could never resist red hair. You were so kind on the trip to Brighton. You brought the Pavilion to life for me – I went on from sixth form to study Art History in London.'

Dan thought for a while, standing still, not dancing. 'Sorry. You mean all those detailed explanations, about Robert Jones's exotic decorating?'

Diana continued to dance, and he followed. 'Yes, you said you were thinking of doing a PhD on him because very little had been written. Did you finish it?'

He shook his head. 'No... sadly not even started. I remember coming to look for you lot on the beach that day... all late back for the train. The boys had stripped off and were paddling... even in autumn. Rather like Cezanne's picture, *The Bathers*.'

Yes, he remembered... the girls had taken their sweaters off and were enjoying the late sunshine in their underwear. He omitted the detail.

Diana laughed at the mention of the boys. 'Yes, they dared *us* to strip but we just took our jumpers off. We could have joined them and been Cezanne's *Three bathers*, the nude women! Silly beggars, such kids, even at eighteen. And we had smuggled tins of booze there. I just picked shells and pebbles – there were some lovely ones.'

*

As the music stopped, before they drew apart, she went on, 'I could have made a fool of myself with you. You reminded me of my dad, so it would have been a very odd affair. Well, not an affair… you were much too decent…' She bit her lip and looked away.

Dan looked at her. 'You were… are… a lovely woman.' He bent and kissed her on the forehead; closing his eyes, he could smell the same fragrance of twenty years before. He wanted to stay in the darkened space.

She looked at him. 'That's what you did when you left us at the station, after we got back from Brighton. Send me a copy when your PhD is published…'

He didn't ask for her address, nor mention the pebble he'd found earlier that evening.

It was nearly eleven and most of the revellers had left, wishing farewells and promises to keep in touch as the party room emptied; the string players slackened their bows; a percussionist released the tension from the drumskin, and the rest packed their instruments away. Dan went through the bar and was greeted by a grin from the barman.

'More time for beer and snooker now? I'll keep an eye on your gifts till tomorrow.'

Dan grinned and pulled his phone from his pocket. Oh God. He'd switched it off when he went on the stage, a missed call from Anne. He phoned the taxi and went to the porch to wait.

No moon now, just dark drizzle and he'd brought no raincoat. He saw the headlights and ran to meet the car.

*

He looked at his phone again: Anne was staying the night at the hospital; her mother had been difficult, so eventually she had been sedated and was sleeping now. She thought the older woman would be distressed to wake up on a ward if Anne weren't there. Dan didn't know whether to laugh or cry. He hadn't drunk much, despite his glass being constantly refilled and now he felt empty and hopeless. He had felt euphoric on the dance floor: Glen Miller's music, her perfume, her warm skin through blue silk and the moon shining through the window had buoyed up his feelings as he held Diana close. She was right. He had always been 'decent' and where had it got him? Where had that young man with the long hair, pink tie, and sneakers, gone? He remembered the poem that had evaded him earlier: 'The Highwayman'. He, Dan, had never been a swashbuckling hero: going for the girl, 'though hell should bar the way'. There had been no 'hell' in his marriage, and he had made a safe choice. He had paid off his mortgage, no job making demands on his time or his health – many a man would envy his good fortune. Over thirty years at the same school: a real stick-in-the-mud. No wonder she had been amazed he was still there.

A Sunday Afternoon in the Garden

Stephanie Ledger

* commended *

It's a lovely sunny day; the first warm, blue-skyed, light-breezed day we've had this year. The first opportunity to spend a lazy Sunday afternoon in the garden. I put the lounger in the dappled shade of the tree and tilt it back. The breeze is refreshing and it stirs the leaves above me. I lean back and look at them gently moving. On this mellow, cloudless Sunday, I find that just watching the patterns of the light as the breeze ruffles the leaves is so relaxing. The slight movement; the changing of greens from light to dark, a glimpse of a silver sliver of sunlight as it slants through the tree is hypnotic.

A bee buzzes in and out of the foxgloves following the trail of purple dots into the lilac centre of the flower to collect the pollen. He emerges, moves onto the next flower, then the next. A busy bee. A buzzy bee. Why do bees buzz? Three small, bright, holly-blue butterflies dance around my head and the perfume of roses creeps in from Neil's garden. A flock of starlings squabble in the tall cedar tree two doors down then scatter to sit in a silent line on the telegraph wires. There are no neighbours being noisy in their gardens today, no traffic, no people passing by in the street. So quiet. So peaceful. Only the soft breeze ruffling the leaves, the sound of birdsong and bees and a faint hum of insects.

I wonder when they'll find the body.

I must have dozed. The sun has moved and is burning into my toes. I go indoors for a book and a glass of water and move my chair back into the shade. The neighbourhood seems to have come to life while I was dozing. Molly's grandchildren are visiting, squealing and shouting as they jump in the paddling pool. They sound as if they are having fun. I wonder if I bought a paddling pool my grandchildren would come and visit me.

Now Neil has got the lawnmower out. Again! I'm surprised there is a blade of grass left standing on his lawn. But the smell of a mown lawn is pleasant, newly cut grass must be one of my favourite smells, it's always the scent of summer.

The noise the children are making has set that yappy little dog at number fifteen off. Yap, yap, yap. I settle down and open the book. Yap, yap, yap.

The blackbird ignores me and continues trying to dig up the bedding plants I've just put in. I usually shoo him off but today my plants seem unimportant.

There are voices from people walking down the street, a car passes. I can tell he's going too fast, it's probably that boy-racer from number thirty-nine.

Faintly in the distance, I can hear the sound of a siren, then it comes closer, the nee-naw, nee-naw getting louder. I listen intently trying to plot its route. It gets nearer and nearer, louder and louder. Every nerve, every muscle in my body tightens. It passes the end of my lane and heads towards the other side of town, not stopping in the next street as I had feared it would. I slowly start to relax again.

They can't have found her body yet.

I'll just sit here and read my book. Or try to read my book. I don't seem able to concentrate, I suppose that's not surprising in the circumstances. I keep rehearsing in my mind what I will say if I'm asked to explain my movements. I'll just say, 'I had a lazy day. I just sat in the garden all afternoon and read my book.' Nosey Jean will confirm that, I've already seen her bedroom curtains twitch a few times, she'll be able to say, 'She just sat in the garden all day, reading her book, or pretending to read it. I think half the time she was asleep.' But isn't that what a person with a clear conscience would do on a sunny Sunday afternoon; relax in the garden, read a book and doze?

Those two lads who have rented the house three doors down are having a barbeque. I can smell the charcoal and the burnt burgers. Their music is a bit loud and it's not really my taste in music; I don't mind though because they're laughing a lot and I love to hear the sound of young people enjoying themselves. Unlike the sound of that bloody dog which is still yapping. The smell of barbequed meat is making me feel hungry but I don't think I have the energy to go into the kitchen and get something to eat. I do feel very lethargic. Maybe it's the heat. Maybe it's a reaction to what happened this morning.

I think it is best if the body isn't found quickly. I seem to remember hearing, or maybe reading in one of those crime books, that the longer away from death the autopsy is the more difficult it is to ascertain the time of death accurately. It's better for me if the time of death is uncertain then I won't have to explain how she was when I left her. Jean will know exactly what time I left her because she saw me coming home.

The smoke and laughter and the music drift over from the lads' barbeque. When was the last time anyone invited me to a barbeque? I can't remember. When was the last time I had a bit of fun? All I seem to have done for the last few years is be at the beck and call of that moaning old bitch. Perhaps now I can look forward to getting my life back. I feel a sudden swelling of joy at the prospect of going out and enjoying myself again. And the money will help.

I wonder who will find her body.

Elaine pops in most evenings just to see if she's alright and needs anything before bed. Although it's Sunday so Elaine might be out for the day. I might have to be the one to find her when I make my usual visit tomorrow morning. I don't want that. I don't know how I'd cope with that. I don't ever want to see her again, dead or alive. Would I manage to be shocked and grief-stricken? Would I be able to cry? Even if the police knocked on the door now would I manage to be upset at the dreadful news? I've got my story ready. I have rehearsed it in my mind but have I over-rehearsed it? Will my responses seem unnatural and stunted? I will say, 'I left her about 11 o'clock, she told me to leave the door unlocked because she had a visitor coming. No, she didn't say who it was, wouldn't tell me who it was, she seemed very secretive. Then I came home and I've just been in the garden all day, just sitting here with my book, dozing a bit, I think.'

'Yes, it is a beautiful day, too beautiful a day for something so tragic to happen.'

Surely only a person who was unaware of the death of

a loved one would laze around in the garden, sunning themselves on a lounger and reading a book. Surely that would be the normal behaviour. Although to be quite honest I don't know what would be considered normal behaviour for someone who has just murdered their mother.

Maybe Elaine will find her. I'm sorry to have to inflict that on Elaine. Elaine can be tiresome, too much the cheery good neighbour, too constantly nice for my liking but she doesn't deserve to have a nasty shock like that. Hopefully, she will just think Mum has died of natural causes. I did arrange Mum to look restful in her chair. I leant her head against a cushion, I pulled the foot rest out and put a blanket over her knees. Maybe I shouldn't have done that. Will they wonder why she had a blanket over her knees when the day is so warm? I know she hasn't been ill, her sight has almost gone and she was a bit wobbly on her legs and she is old. Elaine will think she's just died of natural causes, a heart attack or a stroke or something.

I feel more guilty about upsetting Elaine than I do about killing that vindictive old bat. The world is a better place without my mother. My world is definitely a better place without my mother.

'I'm moving there,' she'd told me this morning pushing a posh brochure towards me, jabbing at the picture on the front with that bony old finger. It was only for the Primrose Nursing Home, the plushest most expensive nursing home in the district. 'Might as well spend my money while I can,' she said, 'have a bit of luxury in my old age, have people who will look after me properly, not half-heartedly and resentfully like you do.' Then when she saw the expression on my face she said, 'Well, there's nobody worth leaving my money too, you don't need it and I'm not letting that useless son of yours get his hands on it. I'm going to spend it all while I still can.'

I thought, actually mother, I do need it. I need some money badly. I don't own my own home. I don't live in a big five-bedroomed house like you; I live in a rented cottage. I just have to exist on benefits. I need whatever bit of money I will inherit from you. I could start to live again, go out, go to the theatre again, go on holiday. Just live without having to count every penny.

But I didn't say that, of course. I didn't give her the pleasure of seeing how much the thought of all that money being frittered away on an expensive nursing home hurt me. She could live for years in that home and then all the money I was hoping to inherit from her would be gone. All the money that I thought would be the compensation for the years of caring for her. Although, this morning I didn't really think of the money I would inherit when she died; it was the more immediate financial problem that was on my mind. If she moved into that nursing home, I wouldn't get the weekly carer's allowance, and I depended on that. I was so angry with her. She was prepared to take even that small amount of money away from me.

I left her sitting in her chair gloating about all the money she was going to spend so I couldn't get my hands on it. I went upstairs, got hold of the biggest pillow I could find, went back down, put it over her face and then leant on it. I'd thought about doing that so many times. Every time she told me how useless I was, how I'd always been dim, how I was plain and unpleasant. How much nicer, kinder, more caring than me was Elaine or the milkman or some random woman in the Co-op. Every time she complained, every time she put me down, every time she demanded that I do something to help her, I fantasised about how easy it would be to take a pillow and push it over her face until she stopped breathing. But it wasn't easy. It seemed to take an awfully long time before her arms stopped trying to claw at me. I could hear a muffled 'please, please, please' as her arms flailed around my head and her feet tried to kick me. Then she said, 'I love you.' At least that is what it sounded like, a very muffled, 'I love you.' Maybe I was wrong, maybe I imagined it because I think I'd waited all my life for her to say that to me. But I couldn't stop then, I couldn't stop to see if she really had said, 'I love you,' I couldn't remove the pillow then, it was too late.

I wonder if they will be able to tell from the autopsy reports that she was suffocated, that she fought to the end. My arm feels sore; I haven't looked to see if I have bruises. I presume they will have to be an autopsy because the death will be unexplained. But she was old, maybe they won't rush to do an autopsy, maybe then it will only be a perfunctory one. Is there such a thing as a perfunctory autopsy? I could Google death by asphyxiation to see what the symptoms are but I suppose that's too late now.

I hope the old bitch hasn't made out a will that leaves everything to a cats' home. It wouldn't be a cats' home though; she hates cats. It's more likely she'd leave everything to the sainted Elaine. She probably thought that Elaine deserved her money more than I did. That would be ironic if I don't inherit a penny from her because I will definitely be losing my £70 a week carer's allowance now. I better search the house tomorrow to see if I can find a will.

Once they have taken the body away.

The sun has gone from the garden now. The sky has clouded over and it's a still balmy evening. Molly's grand-children have gone home, Neil has finished mowing and strimming, chopping and clipping. The lads must have gone down to the pub, their music has stopped and there is just a faint wisp of smoke rising from their cooling barbeque. The smell of the smoke is mingling with the sweet smell of my honeysuckle. The day is gently putting itself to bed, the long grey fingers of a June twilight stretch across the garden, casting shadows deep into the overgrown corners. I don't want to move. I'm just going to sit here and listen to my lovely blackbird singing his heart out.

I wonder if she did say, 'I love you.' After all these years did she really say, 'I love you?'

As the night creeps in, I want to sit here and let the increasing darkness fold its tentacles around me, to envelop me, to hide me from the world. I want the darkness to obliterate the awfulness of everything that has happened today. I want the darkness to obliterate me.

Better Than Netball

Jane Wilson-Howarth

Caving doesn't appeal to everyone but unlike school netball and rounders, it is exciting, invigorating, messy, and pretty much rule-free. Success doesn't depend on being selected for the team; it is an individual thing, yourself against Nature and Nature doesn't care whether you live or die. I thought about that often, serving as a cave rescue warden. Caving satisfied my life-long need to prove myself, and show that women can be as intrepid as men.

I sought out new challenges and decided to push the limits with a round trip within Mendip's longest cave system. Rising at a high point in Somerset, a river mysteriously disappears in the middle of a farmer's field and then crashes and booms through six miles of passages until it joins other subterranean rivers in Wookey Hole. Eventually, it emerges as the River Axe near Wells. Most visitors to Swildon's Hole follow the river down through the cave until the roof comes down so low that continuing means diving through an underwater passage – a sump. Few go any further.

The trip I wanted to do involved free-diving, not just this one, but three flooded passages in all. I am a strong swimmer and, in a pool, can manage a length underwater so although the longest sump is 33 feet and rated 'difficult', I thought I could do it. I knew the first person to have free-dived this sump. He was a cave-SCUBA-diver. He hadn't planned to do any free-diving but found himself on the wrong side of the sump having used up all his bottled air, earning him the nickname of Fish in the process. When I talked to him about attempting it, he was discouraging but perhaps he didn't want his achievement eclipsed through being repeated by a mere woman.

John, a regular caving partner, and I donned battered wet suits, climbing boots, helmets and miners' lamps and scrambled awkwardly down between a collection of slick black boulders. Soon though we could stand upright and follow clear bubbling water down a series of beautifully sculpted corridors decorated by gleaming white stalactites and translucent calcite curtains. Oddly, caves don't seem like dark places because helmet-mounted lights ensure that everywhere we look is brightly lit, until things go wrong.

At weekends the first part of the cave is often crowded with less experienced adventurers. The Forty-Foot Drop is often a pinch point. Here, the clear stream looks like a salmon river as it powers over a sheer edge and rumbles away into the depths. Most cavers descend the drop using a portable steel and wire ladder, but we'd discovered routes to free-climb this particular impediment.

We moved between shivering boy scouts while John, chatty as ever, said chuckling, 'Did I tell you? I was called out by the Police last Sunday night. Two young lads had gone into the cave with black rubber torches and hadn't come out. The batteries had died after a couple of hours, no doubt. The boys were here, quivering with cold, at the bottom of the waterfall. I threw down the safety rope and shouted, "Tie on! Then climb the ladder." I heard from below, "Where do we tie the rope?" I wanted to get back to my pint and shouted down my reply, "Where do you think? Round your fucking neck!"

Finally, I felt the rope give as the first boy climbed up. His head appeared over the lip of the waterfall and – I'm not kidding – he had the rope tied around his fucking neck!'

'Seriously!' I said. 'You couldn't make it up, eh?' and I slid over the edge of the waterfall. I found a jug-hold out over the drop, felt with my feet until they found a ledge and swung in through the sparkling water. Once under the cascade, a series of easy moves got me to the bottom. Meanwhile, long lean John had straddled the little subterranean canyon and danced down the rockface like Spiderman.

Invigorated, we splashed on through ankle-deep water, our boots crunching on ivory-coloured pebbles and pieces of crystal. We jogged along corridors with walls composed of fossil seashells and coral. Everything was so pristine I wanted to stop and admire the wonderful patterns in the rocks and a pool of cave pearls. While John expertly climbed down the Twenty-Foot Pot, I ran my fingers over the strata and flowstone formations that looked like icing. The next landmark was the Twin Pots where double waterfalls dropping 15 feet or so have rattled boulders around in circles to form two perfectly round bath-tubs. Two young men were edging around the rims of each pot but we knew that the water was free of boulders and only chest deep so, exuberant still, we jumped in with satisfying whoops, splashing both lads just a little. This was Type One fun.

Laughing still, we separated. John was an excellent caver and, unlike me, was cool climbing sheer rock-faces, but he definitely wasn't keen on water so I left him to continue down the main channel to Sump 1 where he'd wait for me. My route now involved a meandering climb above the river, taking an unfamiliar direction that circled around and above this first sump to rejoin the river perhaps half a mile downstream. Then navigating upstream again I would need to negotiate three submerged passages before I met up with John again.

I scrambled up into higher passages that were seldom river-washed: there was more mud and less shine but I felt intrepid. I liked being totally alone for a while. I especially loved visiting places few others had been. After the next big scramble, I sat to get my breath back, raising my own personal steam-clouds with each exhalation. I switched off my light to absorb the strangeness of total blackness.

Eyes wide open, scanning this way and that, there was not even the subtlest of shadows. Nothing. Not a glimmer. Nowhere on the surface of this planet can you experience such a total absence of light. In such absolute blackness the mind hallucinates sparks and shapes.

I recalled a friend whose light had failed and he tried to navigate using occasional flashes from his camera but although the flashes lit up whole chambers he couldn't navigate these images in his mind as he tried to move through the cave. Eventually, bewildered, he sat and waited until we rescued him. Another friend did manage to find his way back to the cave entrance just by the orange light of a cigarette. With his eyes accustomed to blackness, dragging on the cigarette allowed him to see the details of the chambers and corridors he was moving through.

I listened in the blackness. I was too far above the river now to be able to hear it, or anything going on in the world above. There were subtle sounds of the cave breathing. There was perhaps a distant flutter of bat wings. Otherwise, there was only the slow drip, drip, dripping as drops collecting in cracks in the cave roof or on the tips of stalactites fell into pools or onto rocks. This was true sensory deprivation.

I shivered. My butt-cheeks were numb. Cold was seeping into me. I checked my emergency glow-stick was still safely tucked up inside my wetsuit near my calf, switched on my cap-lamp and headed onwards.

Maybe half an hour later, I heard the river again. I'd arrived in a medium-sized chamber at the top of another descent. Others had described this landmark, and it was good to know that I was on track. This drop was 15 or 20 feet but at an angle of only about 30°, so going down should have been easy. The surface though was a water-smoothed slab of limestone that was covered with cave-clay. It was soap-slippery but I wasn't going to edge down on all fours.

I was all-too-aware of the danger even of an ankle sprain this far underground. Hypothermia soon sets in and people die but I was exhilarated and threw caution to the wind, launching myself with a manic shriek, which echoed back at me as I joyously hurtled down the face of the slab. I'd started to slide feet-first but spun on the descent so rejoined the river below with a spectacular but inelegant splash. I was still laughing and feeling slightly dizzy as I scrambled to my feet. I registered a slightly bruised left buttock, but was pleased to have reached the main river again. I turned to head upstream.

It wasn't long before I reached the first of the three sumps I'd need to swim. This, Sump 3, was the one rated 'free-divable but difficult'. This was the one Fish had discouraged me from attempting, and now I was here, 33 feet was indeed an intimidating distance. I was determined though. Maybe I'd be the first woman to free-dive it.

As expected, there was a decent-looking rope tied via a bolt in the rock at my end and I pulled to check that the other end was secure too. Churned-up sediments would stop me seeing much – if anything. Nor did I know if there was scope for turning around if anything went wrong.

There was no point in thinking too much about this though. That would only make me feel even more anxious than I already was. I took steady breaths and then a really deep one and plunged in.

My helmet clattered against rock. My wetsuit made me too buoyant, sticking me to the uneven cave roof. I felt for the battery at my waist, checking. I tried pushing off the rocks with my boots but that didn't help. This wasn't going to be a smooth easy swim. I thrashed. I struggled to unpeel myself from jagged protrusions in the cave roof. Then, finally, I settled for pulling myself along the rope while on my side, fending off the roof with my elbow. I still crashed into rock a lot but I was making progress – not good progress, but some progress.

How far had I gone? All I could see was a mud-coloured blur. My helmet rattling on the cave roof made a lot of noise. I needed to get to air soon. Maybe I should turn back.

There was supposed to be an airbell part way but could I find it? Or was that in the other sump? Best continue. I pulled and pulled. I had a feeling I'd put my fist up into air but wasn't sure. I pulled and concentrated on nothing but that. My need to breathe was becoming dire. I pulled some more and finally exploded to the surface, and air.

Shaking water from my face and head, I took a huge, wheezing in-breath. I choked and spat water. I found somewhere I could get my feet down. Stood. Hit my helmeted head on the cave roof. I panted, hands on hips, waist-deep in turbid water, feeling sick.

I calmed my breathing. I surged out onto a rocky beach and stood shakily looking back at the pool I'd just emerged from.

I pulled myself together. There was no point hanging around.

I strode on, further upstream, and soon came to the next sump.

I didn't want to go on but now there was no choice. I was on my own, in a place I had never been before, between two long flooded passages, dependent on my one light. I was scared but now I had to swim my way out under water with no hope of surfacing if anything went wrong.

Once again there was a bolt securing a stout-looking rope that disappeared into muddy water. Sump 2 was supposedly easier than Sump 3, at 26 feet long. The best route home was to dive this one and finally the much shorter Sump 1 which I had swum through several times before. John was waiting on the far side.

My heart was hammering. I knew I mustn't hesitate. Anticipation always makes things worse. I checked my battery pack on my belt, that my light was secure on my helmet and boot laces tied. I was procrastinating. I tried to swallow down my fear. Again, I took some breaths, then a really big one and dived in. This sump seemed narrow. I crashed into the roof, and the cave wall to my left.

I was so scared of letting go of the rope I ended up with a loop clutched in my two hands. Just pull, I told myself. I fended off the roof with my right elbow again. There was solid rock to my right. My helmet rattled. I pulled. The world was a muddy blur. I was progressing forwards. How far now? More pulling. Feeling short of air. Needing to breathe. Onwards, endlessly pulling on the rope, scrabbling with my boots. Then finally I was in air. I staggered out of the water again, shaky-legged. I didn't pause to get my breath back. All that was in my mind was getting out of this cave.

I splashed onwards, jogging now, relieved I'd conquered the big challenges. Soon the pool that was Sump 1 was in sight. Someone had placed a stolen street sign there. It read,

Wookey Hole 1½ miles
avoiding town centre

At that moment I didn't care about cavers' pranks, threw myself in and swam through. So easy. I surfaced and scanned around. Someone was crouched on a rock. When he saw me, he switched on his light and said, 'All right?'

'Yeah', and I stumbled over and hugged him. I needed human contact.

He pulled out a squashed Mars Bar from somewhere.

I said, 'John, you absolute star!'

'Yeah,' he said, 'I know how to treat a lady!'

We shared the chocolate and headed back to the surface, peeled off wetsuits and made for the Hunters Lodge Inn. There, I downed a pint or two of Somerset rough cider, regaled my caving mates with tales of my intrepidtude, and savoured some Type Two fun.

© Jane Wilson-Howarth, 2024

Darkness by Design

Jane Phillips

Night fell and so did I.

A long fall and apparently no broken bones or the slightest pain. I had no idea how long I'd been here, but who would have thought that dying could be that easy?

I picked myself up and looked all round. A tunnel in front and a dead end behind. A one-way ticket then, and, at the end, Heaven, Hell or, most probably, Nothing. I looked for the Grim Reaper but he, she or they (we must be inclusive these days) wasn't in attendance. Poor show, that.

As I searched for something to light my way, a small nun popped out of the shadows. She looked me up and down, no mean feat as she had to adjust her wimple to stretch her neck backwards in order to see my face. She beamed up at me. 'Oh, how lovely! I haven't accompanied a young one for ages. And so tall too. Come on. This way.' And she marched ahead into the tunnel.

Stupified, I had no choice but to follow. 'Come on, come on,' she called. 'Don't dawdle or we'll be late for the flight.'

I hurried to catch up with her. 'Excuse me, but are you DEATH? I must say I'd assumed a tall person with a stooped back wearing a black cloak and carrying a scythe on his shoulder.' I quickly added, 'Or her or their, as you prefer.'

The nun turned and giggled. 'Just go for what you want dear. We're not overly worried about being gender-specific here.' She smiled a beautiful smile. Her face, already soft, softened further. 'And no, I'm not DEATH, but thank you for the compliment. You know that Nicholas has those little elves, well, DEATH has a band of helpers too. We're mostly nuns. It's the black habits.' She did an un-nunlike twirl. 'I'm told they're in keeping with the overall design strategy.' She breathed a long sigh. 'DEATH is so busy, what with all that's going on in the world. Now, step lively, we've got some way to go. And mind the puddles.'

That was when I realised that, though the darkness was all-embracing, I could see my way. 'Like Nightcrawler.'

I hadn't realised I'd spoken aloud until the nun replied, 'And I bet you wish you could teleport too. Never mind, dear. You can't. You must see that it would be dangerous, far, far too dangerous. It could get you back out of here and we couldn't have that. No return tickets from this destination. But cheer up, dear. One of your superhero qualities will be tested soon enough.'

I could feel the darkness all around, hugging me tight. It wasn't unpleasant, more like a warm, furry blanket than a damp fog. It was the blackest black I'd ever encountered but still I could see through it. How was that possible? I would have to ask the nun.

'Excuse me, Sister. This darkness envelopes us, but I can see through it. I don't understand.'

'I know dear – and you a physicist and all. Let's just

say that the laws of physics don't apply here in the same way as they do in during-life.'

'Injuring life?'

'Sorry, dear. They keep telling me I shouldn't chew gum while I'm escorting. During-life – it's what we call the time before after-life. After-life is where you're going now.'

'How come you know I'm a physicist?'

I didn't think nuns said, 'Duh!'

'Duh!' she said. 'We know all about you. Well, nearly all. That's why the test. Most people go straight to the correct departure lounge. There's a bit of a query over you. Hence the final test.'

'So, can you give me any clues – anything to help me?'

'Good Lord, no. That would be cheating and you can't cheat death, you know.'

Made sense. 'Death and taxes.'

Again, I felt I hadn't spoken aloud, but the nun laughed. 'Taxis, you won't get a taxi down here. Had to stop them when the designers insisted that they couldn't use lights. And anyway, we're nearly at the next stage.' She made an expansive gesture with her hands. 'And just look at this. Those design people decided that the darkness here should be just a little bit less embracing. What do you think? Seems a bit OTT to me to have an arbitrary change in darkness, but they were quite insistent. Said it added texture. Anyway, dear, this is where I leave you.'

We were in a small room full of office equipment. It was my office at the university, except that this one had no doors and no windows. She pointed to the space in front of us. 'You need to get through one of the walls. Good luck!' She turned and faded into the background – black on black – and disappeared.

I stood for a while as the enveloping darkness slowly transformed itself into a swirling grey. It reminded me of the early morning mists on the Fens. But this was a dry grey, less familiar than Fenland fog. Tears came to my eyes as I realised I would never again be able to take an early morning run on the flat lands around Cambridge.

Steeling myself to adopt a positive mental attitude, I wiped my eyes and looked for a wall without any obstacles such as desks or filing cabinets. Then I tested it for solidity. It was stud partitioning, typical of public buildings, solid but with a small amount of give. I stepped back a few yards and then took a run at the wall.

The shock was severe but I felt no pain, only the ignominy of finding myself sitting on the same office floor and, quite literally, seeing stars. No blood that I could see, nothing to suggest anything was broken and, when the stars subsided, still no pain. And certainly nothing to suggest that I was ever going to master the fourth dimension, or whichever dimension I had landed in. I had expected to be subject to the laws of after-life physics, but it seemed that, in my case, during-life physics still prevailed.

I found an empty chair. Beside it was a book; *The Creation And Dispersal Of Human Energy*. My magnum opus, the one that had made my fame and fortune. I opened it, thinking that it might help me to understand my disembodied state. Part One was entitled 'Where It Comes From', Part Two, 'Where It Goes' and Part Three was headed 'What No-one Knows'. So far so good. A small pink bookmark rested within part three. I turned to that page and began to read.

The letters danced before me, moving in and out of the ethereal mists. I groaned. 'Oh, don't tell me this book is laden with mystic powers that only the thoroughly dead can see.' I liked facts. I might be on the dead side of alive but that shouldn't get in the way of reality. I fumbled in my pocket, found my handkerchief and wiped my glasses. The mists cleared and I started again.

"Human energy is a self-contained cosmic matrix, loaded with positive, negative and neutral nodes in an ever shifting diamorphic network of radiative matter."

I stopped reading. This was drivel. How had I managed to mislead people all this time? I hoped that, now that I was dead, someone would be brave enough to see the Emperor for what he was – not naked but a fool who had bamboozled them all.

'You're right, that book's rubbish!' The same little old lady. In my seated state, I was at eye level with her. She looked straight at me and grinned. 'You need this instead,' and she vanished just as quickly as she'd appeared. In her place was a small map. I felt loath to trust something donated by a vanishing nun, but then I suspected that I didn't have much choice. Being in this deserted office with only a map for company was a worse blow than being dead; at least that was logical! A fatalist control-freak finds it hard to deal with surprises and hand-drawn maps. Especially, when they are drawn in bright pink ink.

The map was of a hospital. Well, almost. It was as if the original map had been overlaid with a map of a completely different hospital. The words 'Dead Zone' in bright fuchsia highlighted whole new areas. I stood up, put the book back where I'd found it and headed in the general direction of the Dead Zone through a door that definitely had not been there earlier.

The directions on the map were surprisingly easy to follow and I soon found myself standing before a desk marked Departures. The designers had been at their most creative here. This large area managed to be in twilight at one end with the light level increasing into the distance. The far end – at least a football pitch away – was bathed in full sunlight. As the whole was covered by a solid roof, this intrigued me. The physics here was obviously of the after-life sort.

In my past life, I had often been invisible to people at reception desks, so, in the anticipation of being totally ignored, I looked at the receptionist and smiled my most winning smile.

The receptionist smiled back. 'Welcome to the departure lounge. I'd just like to check a few details and then we can start you on your journey. Alex Smith; died, let's see, nearly twelve hours ago. My, but it's taken you a while to get here. Now tell me, why is that?'

I was more than usually dumbfounded. I had no idea what was happening. I had the distinct impression that this was a moment of truth and I didn't want to get it wrong. Eternity was a long time. 'No.' My pedantry forced me to add, 'time has no value in eternity'. But that didn't make it any easier. I stuttered, 'Er, I'm not sure. There was a nun and a test, and I'm not even sure that I've passed. But I do know that I can't go back and right the wrongs I've left behind – and that bugs me. Um, is there a helpdesk I could go to?'

The receptionist sat up. 'That's a perfect response for proceeding to Cloud 9.' She pointed to my left. 'This small nun will show you the way.'

I looked down at the nun. Of course, it was the same one.

The receptionist handed me my ticket and continued, 'When you arrive at Cloud 9, you will be met by a Guardian who will accompany you on your journey and explain your position in the Heavenly Host. Have a nice death. Next please!'

I looked long and hard at the nun. She grinned up at me.

I smiled back. 'Okay,' I said. 'Why the delay, and the one that really bugs me, why bright pink ink?'

Now the grin was beatific. 'You were one of those cases which could go either way so it was a test. We need people in Heaven who know their limitations and repent their wrongdoings. And we're desperate for more scientists. So I was sent here to fast-track you.' She led me to a row of airport seats and sat down heavily. 'Such a pity that so many of you science people are unbelievers. Agnostics, we can deal with pretty quickly. But full, dyed-in-the-wool athiests take aeons to process, so we have a science backlog. We're having to house them in limbo while we process them. Such a waste. In the meantime, we're over-run by creatives. Those darkness designers are just the tip of the iceberg. We're unbalanced and that will never do.' She laid her hand on mine. Her touch was as light as featherdown. 'And why pink, you ask? Number one, it's not black. Number two, it's my very favourite colour. Now, let's go and meet your angel. I know you'll like him.'

© Jane Phillips, 2024

Gotcha!

Les Brookes

* commended *

When the lights went out, Paul was kissing Adam in the cupboard under the stairs and Todd was fondling Anna's breasts behind the locked door of the spare room. The music from the sound system died and there was a moment of stunned silence. Then a great howl went up from the guests in the sitting room.

'Oh hell!' squealed Maggie in the kitchen. 'A power cut!'

'Aaagh!' groaned her husband, Steve. 'Just what we need.'

'Yeah,' she said. 'Brilliant timing!'

They were loading the kitchen table with triangular sandwiches, *vol-au-vents*, crisps, olives, celery sticks and pineapple kebabs. He thrust a bowl under her nose as if another prawn cracker might compensate. There was just enough light from the radiant moon to see by.

Greta appeared at the door, face and shoulders drooping.

'Oh Dad!' she wailed. 'Bang goes my eighteenth.'

He stepped forward and hugged her, and there was general lamentation before Maggie made a quick, brave recovery.

'Candles,' she said.

'But where?' said Steve.

'Eh… not sure… under the stairs… I think.'

Steve found his phone, snapped on the torch, and went in search. He beamed around, stumbled over boxes, cursed several times, and eventually found what he was looking for, the beam, by the merest fluke, missing Paul and Adam crouched in a far corner.

He returned with a hundred tea lights in a box. '*Gott sei Dank!*' breathed Maggie, who taught German and had spent a year in Munich. They lit a couple of dozen and placed them on tables and ledges in all parts of the house.

'Sorry, everyone,' said Steve, addressing the guests. 'Not *my* doing.'

'No problem,' shrugged Ben. 'That music was crap anyway.'

'Oh thanks,' quipped Andy, the acting DJ.

'Anyway,' said Sonia, 'let there be light. And soon.'

'Oh no,' sighed Prue. 'I *love* candlelight. It's so romantic.'

Soppy twit, thought Bob.

Maggie, clapping her hands, called everyone to the table for refreshments. Bob, thickset and pushy, was first off the mark and piled his plate high. There were cartons of juice, some bottles of wine, and everyone was urged to go easy on the punch. Grouping themselves around Andy, who had brought his guitar, they squatted on the floor and sang between bites.

In the middle of this diversion there was a loud clack on the knocker of the front door and Greta went to answer. No one there. Just a radiant moon in a clear sky. She stepped into the street and glanced around. Not a soul to be seen. She shrugged. But as she turned to go back in something flashed in the corner of her eye. She turned again and saw a figure standing on the other side of the street. He'd appeared, it seemed, from nowhere.

'Hullo,' she called. 'Was that you? Did you knock?'

The young man came across. Tall, blond, handsome. She winced at the near-cliché, but the tag came instantly to mind and was unavoidable.

'No, not me,' he said, with the trace of an accent. 'I'm just passing. Taking a walk. It's no fun sitting in the dark, is it?'

She smiled. 'And you didn't see anyone?'

'No,' he said. 'I stopped because I heard the music.'

'It's my birthday,' she said. 'We're having a party.'

'Oh really?' His eyes widened. 'Happy birthday!'

'Thank you,' she giggled. 'So do you live around here?'

'I've just arrived from Germany. I'm a student. I'm a bit lost. I don't know anyone.'

She paused. The poor young man. Did she dare invite him in? But why not? He was perfectly charming. And what's more he had a glint in his eye that made her heart flutter.

'Oh, don't feel lost. Come inside and join us.' She ushered him in. 'It's a bit makeshift, I'm afraid. Songs by candlelight.' She led him through the hall. 'What's your name, by the way?'

'It's Johann, but everyone calls me Hans.'

'I'm Greta,' she murmured.

34

She waved him into the kitchen and introduced him to her parents.

'*Willkommen*,' trilled Maggie, before addressing him in fluent German. Then, turning to Greta and Steve, 'He comes from Munich. Isn't that extraordinary? He wants to know my impression of it.'

'Amazing,' said Greta, gazing at her protégé in awe. 'Now, Hans, come and meet the others.' She led him into the sitting room. 'Andy, this is Hans.' The two young men shook hands, eyeing each other with hints of suspicion. 'Andy is my boyfriend,' she smirked.

When the introductions were over, Andy resumed playing and singing, and Hans squatted on the floor with a glass of wine opposite Greta. Everyone joined in the choruses, including Hans, who quickly picked up the words. He had a deep, sonorous voice that made Greta's spine tingle, and whenever she looked at him he was gazing back at her with eyes that flashed in the candlelight. Were they green? She recalled reading somewhere that green eyes are not uncommon, especially in people from central Europe.

'Steve, can you fetch some tea-towels?' said Maggie in the kitchen.

He nodded, but as he mounted the stairs he heard movement. He peered over the bannister and saw Paul and Adam creeping from the cupboard beneath. They entered the kitchen and when he returned they were squatting on the sitting room floor with plates of sandwiches and singing along with the others.

He delivered the towels and stood gazing at the floor. 'Maggie,' he said, 'no big deal... but have you ever thought that our son might be... well, you know... gay?'

'Of course I have.'

'So, why haven't I?'

'Because men are obtuse.'

At this moment, smack on cue, Paul and Adam appeared in the doorway holding hands. They stood for some moments, looking nervously intent, their eyes fixed on Maggie and Steve. Then Paul drew a deep breath.

'Mum, Dad,' he gulped, 'we've something to tell you.'

This announcement was interrupted by a crash in the sitting room, followed by an uproar. They all went to investigate and found Andy glaring at Hans, who was mopping his nose with a napkin. Bob and Mike were holding them apart, but Andy soon slunk off and flopped in a corner. Greta went to console him.

'Him or me?' he growled.

'Don't be silly,' she crooned, kissing his cheek.

But he couldn't be persuaded to take up his guitar again, and the guests turned to each other at a loss. What now? There were shrugs and dispirited looks all around.

'Perhaps we could play a game,' suggested Sonia.

'Like what?'

'Hide and seek?'

'What, in the dark?'

'Yeah, really scary in the dark. Anyone like to hide? Indoors or out. But somewhere within a hundred yards.'

Greta, feeling guilty about the disruption and keen to save the evening, volunteered.

'Okay, Greta, you have just one minute to hide. Anyone who finds her should shout *Gotcha!* Everyone back here in fifteen minutes, found or not.'

They all shut their eyes and blocked their ears. Greta left by the front door and crossed the street. She crawled into the concrete cylinder in the children's play area and lay prone, her heart beating, and after a while she heard footsteps. A shadow appeared at the entrance, then a pair of flashing green eyes. She stifled a scream.

'Boo!' came a deep, sonorous voice. 'Gotcha!'

Fifteen minutes later everyone except Greta and Hans was back in the sitting room.

'Give a shout,' said Sonia. 'Tell them to come in.'

Andy went outside and yelled.

No response.

'Jesus, where the hell are they?' he fumed.

'Yeah,' growled Bob, 'and who the hell is that guy?'

'Someone she found in the street,' said Sonia.

Ten minutes later, the pair were still missing and there was now feverish concern. Andy reported the disappearance to Greta's parents in the kitchen. Maggie turned to Steve with a face like chalk.

'Oh God!' she muttered, slapping her brow. 'How could I forget? It's *Walpurgisnacht*.'

'Val who?' he said.

'Oh, you know – in Goethe's *Faust* – the Witches' Sabbath.'

'Maggie, our daughter is missing and you're wittering on about Goethe?'

'Steve, the date of her birth. It's always troubled me. Tonight, people in Germany light fires and sing songs to repel evil spirits.'

'Oh, for God's sake! Are you seriously suggesting…?'

Andy glared at them both, threw up his hands and stormed off into the sitting room. 'I'm going to look for her,' he announced to the guests. 'Anyone join me?'

A couple of hands shot up, then a few more, until

finally all hands were raised.

At the door Andy addressed the search party. 'If you find her, shout *Eureka!* Otherwise back here in twenty minutes.'

Maggie urged everyone to stay in pairs and keep their distance. She gave Andy a cricket bat, Bob a crowbar. They gaped at her as if she were insane but didn't argue.

'Take your phones, all of you,' she urged. 'Steve and I will stay here and call you if Greta returns.'

The group spread out, Andy and Bob taking the lower road. The street lighting was off, but there was ample moonlight as well as the torchlight from their phones. They passed through the streets calling Greta by name, and sometimes a curtain twitched, though all the houses were in darkness and they met no one. They heard the others calling in the streets around, their voices hard and dry in the clear air.

After fifteen minutes Andy looked at his watch. 'Time to turn back,' he said.

Then, a few yards from the house, he glanced across the street. He pulled up short and gripped Bob by the arm. Someone was sitting on a swing in the children's play area gazing at the ground. They ran across and Greta raised her head as they approached. She looked confused and distressed.

Andy cradled her face in his hands. 'Where've you been, love?'

She stared. 'I… don't know.'

'You don't *know*?'

Her lips trembled. 'I… don't remember.'

The men exchanged looks of alarm.

'Have you seen Hans?'

Her brow wrinkled. 'Who?' she asked.

Andy threw another look at Bob, shook his head, and took her by the arm.

'Come on, love, we're going home,' he said.

In the house, her parents hugged her, sat her down, and brought her a hot drink. She sat in silence while the guests made a fuss of her, plying her with questions that she met with a blank look.

'Leave her be,' said Maggie. 'She's had a shock. I'm putting her to bed.'

The guests stayed a little longer, then started to drift away; the party was clearly over. Andy alone remained, sitting at her bedside, holding her hand. She lay staring at the ceiling, though sometimes she turned to face him. She seemed changed – or was it the effect of the candlelight? Her slate eyes glistened, and sometimes he thought he caught a flash of green. Was that his fancy, or his memory of the light in Hans's eyes when he gazed at her? Whatever the case, he had to get a grip. This eerie sense of menace, this prickling of his skin, was Maggie's doing and quite ridiculous. She'd spooked him. He was furious with her. Her talk of witches was hysterical. And then her name-dropping. I mean, who the fuck is Goethe?

He left at two in the morning, just as the lights came back on, and hurried home, hoping to snatch a few hours of sleep. He looked around for Hans but saw no one.

Greta was in bed for ten days, complaining of tiredness, sickness, and mysterious ailments. Andy came to see her daily, and when she began to recover he questioned her gently. So what happened that night, love? Did you hear me calling? Why didn't you return? She had no answers; she seemed to have lost all memory of it.

Then, four weeks later, having missed her period, she took a pregnancy test and stared in shock at the result. She lived with her secret for a week before breaking it to Andy. He gazed at her in silence for several minutes. Then he kissed and hugged her. 'Hey, don't be down, love,' he beamed. 'It's wonderful news. We should get hitched as soon as possible.'

Her parents, however, were less than thrilled. 'Could be worse,' said Maggie, when they were alone. 'Andy's a decent bloke.'

'Oh, I like Andy,' said Steve, 'but the world is spinning too fast for me. I mean, in the past few weeks I've learned that my son is gay, my daughter pregnant, my wife a ghoul-chaser.'

'Oh Steve, just get over yourself. We've other fish to fry.'

He shook his head, wandered to the window and stood gazing into the garden. 'You know, I can't help thinking about that night,' he mused. 'I mean, have you ever wondered what happened to Hans? He's never been seen since.'

'Have I ever wondered!' she scoffed.

The baby, a beautiful boy, arrived on time. He had Greta's blond hair and slate eyes, and a hint of her snub nose. Steve viewed him with delight; Maggie studied him with a troubled smile; Andy cradled him, searching his face. But when their eyes locked, he started. For there it was again: that flash of green. His scalp tingled. He shook his head and refocused. He had to snap out of this. He was again falling prey to Maggie's silliness. There was nothing to be alarmed about. Green eyes were common, weren't they? Indeed, Greta had a touch – though admittedly he'd not noticed till the night of the party. He handed the child back to Greta, and smiled at them both. How alike they looked, right down to that flash in the eyes.

The visitors turned to each other. 'We should go,' said Maggie. 'She must be tired.'

They kissed her, moved to the door and waved. Greta was propped up, the boy in her arms. It was a scene of biblical serenity. All it needs, thought Andy, is the shepherds and the Magi.

© Les Brookes, 2024

Grotesque Nature

Stephen Port-Burke

Mary Woodbridge was not happy walking out of the District Council Offices in Ely. They were as useless as her dead husband. It wasn't right. Her caravan had been pitched in that spot along the spine of the River Ouse for over 30 years, and now they were telling her she needed to move, apply for housing, leave Dobbie, her chickens, her vegetable garden, and her lovely orchard she worked so hard to cultivate behind for some new local business that acquired the land and wanted her evicted.

Of course, she knew she could draw it out in court proceedings that she knew would never rule in her favour, and a solicitor cost money. She only earned some extra money as a hedge witch selling the magical herbs she gathered, and the magical charms she made, along with the potions she concocted to the Roma tribes living in Earith, and Wentworth, and other tribes passing through now and again, and some of the people living in the local villages. She also did a bit of midwifery, but that was often paid in labour, helping her patch Dobbie's stable, her caravan, and, if not that, someone helped her till the soil, which always made her back ache, especially, now that she was in her seventies.

Mary walked with her satchel to have lunch at Ely Cathedral while she waited for Jacques who offered to take her back home after he peddled some of the carvings and trinkets he crafted down by the Market, and down by the Riverfront. It was busy this week with the Art Festival and weather being nice.

Surprisingly, she found an unoccupied bench and sat down for lunch, taking out her egg sandwich mixed with nettles, which she added to help her aching joints.

While she ate and soaked up the sun, she listened to a husband groan about the heat and climate change, and wondered if she could find a loophole around the Council's decision. She would have to ask some of the Romas if they had any suggestions or ideas. Why couldn't they just leave her alone? She wasn't causing any problems. She found peace living out in the Fens after the hell her husband had put her through, treating her like a slave, beating her, and forcing himself on her whenever he wanted a poke.

She knew she was riling herself and knew it wasn't going to help matters, so she set her eyes upon the Cathedral, a comforting presence in her life, and thought about all the times she climbed the embankment at night, to get away from her husband, to find solace in the Cathedral's beacon of light that reached out to her across the countryside.

The Cathedral stored powerful magic. If only she could access the magic to help her. There were ways, she knew, but dwelling in dark magic had its consequences and she already suffered enough for a lifetime, *why should you suffer more?* The voice entered her head. She looked around at the families having picnics on the grass, and the couples strolling by, and looked at the teenage boy who just sat down next to her texting away on his phone.

'Boy. Did you say something?'

The boy looked at her as though she was crazy. 'No,' and walked away.

Mary wondered if she was going senile, but it was true, *why should you suffer more?*

Jacques dropped her off at her caravan in the mid afternoon and she paid him with a sack of her vegetables before he trotted off in his cart. She would need his services again.

She took a moment to bask some more in the sunshine to soothe her aching joints, before she went about her chores, checking on Dobbie first, the chickens, the garden, the voice a constant presence in her thoughts, but what could she do?

After a simple dinner of rabbit stew, she pottered about, mending a button on a shirt, washing clothes and hanging them out to dry, before climbing the embankment on the well-trodden path she had made over the years. She sat up there on an old camping chair she had saved from the tip years ago, gazing at Ely Cathedral's lights and pondered some more over the voice, before heading back down for the night.

Sleep didn't come easy. She was worried. She didn't want to give up her home, Dobbie, and her little patch of peace she created here, and in the darkest hours of sleep, the grotesque approached her in the dreamy mist, his voice entering her mind, *why should you suffer more?*

His ebony skin, and feline body, sleek and muscular, entranced her, but it was his human face, elongated and contorted like a serpent, with fangs protruding and smirking at her discomfort behind a hedgerow of greasy facial hair that made her take a step back clutching her mirrored charm hanging around her neck.

The darkness enfolded her, and his whispers transcended with her, why should you suffer more… why should you suffer more… free us from our stone prisons… seek our help… it has always been the way of the Romas and the grotesques since dragons were born… seek our help… we are your servants…

The next day Mary entered the Village Hall. She walked past a wall displaying 'Save the Planet' artwork made by the local children and past a group of middle-aged men and women performing yoga on different coloured yoga mats, and spoke to Laura sitting at the table in the back room.

Laura was a retired nurse and kindred spirit who volunteered on occasions to monitor the Village Hall during the daytime. Mary enjoyed having tea with her when she came down to the Village Hall, whenever she had need of the phone. They exchanged pleasantries and when Mary asked politely to use the phone, Laura willingly handed it over, 'Of course, love.'

Mary dialled the solicitor's number the Council Officer gave her, and queued for over thirty minutes, listening to the repeating song, the pause, and the message, *We are experiencing a high volume of calls. A representative will be with you shortly, or visit our government website at www…*

She hung up, 'Donkey asses!' She didn't even own a computer. She knew the system was run by weasels promising to help. They would tell her to call this person, and that person will tell her to call the person she just talked too, in an endless cycle of doing absolutely nothing. All of them as useless as her dead husband. Why did she bother? She already knew they weren't going to help someone like her, but she had to try. The grotesque in her dreams disturbed her. Grotesques were demons, chimeras, tricksters, and their intentions were usually of a dark nature

Mary politely refused tea with Laura and apologised.

Laura gave her a look of concerned disappointment, 'Is everything okay, love?'

'No.' Mary explained she had some matters to sort with the council.

'Wish you luck with that, love.' Laura mumbled something about a past grievance she had with the council.

Mary bid Laura farewell, and headed back to her caravan, the grotesque's voice a travelling companion on her conscious.

On her way back, vans were strewn across the meadow she liked to stroll through. Deep ruts marked their intrusion, and an excavator was digging up the precious earth where many of the herbs she gathered grew, and was ruining the wild strawberry patch she cherished. 'Those knob-gobblers,' she cursed them.

She walked furiously past. She had enough. She knew those bureaucrats didn't need the patch of land she lived on and could have left her alone. This was about insurance costs and liability. Well, she was liable for herself. They needn't worry, but she knew they were cowards, afraid she might sue them if she ever got hurt on the land they now owned, even if she signed a legal document safeguarding them from any incidents that may occur, but that would incur costs and these bureaucrats liked to keep their pockets bulging to disguise their puny pricks.

At home she made a cup of tea to settle her nerves, and sat outside her caravan, remembering the tales told by her elders around the campfires during her youth, about

Romas who took great risks conjuring demons, such as the grotesque in her dream, enslaving them, making them servants, and extorting their powers to obtain riches and powers beyond belief, but there were always warnings attached to these tales, consequences for the Roma who didn't keep a tight noose around their servants throat.

In some ways she sympathised with these demons. She had felt like a servant with a noose around her neck most of her married life with her husband. She weighed the risks. Dark magic wasn't forbidden by the Roma. There were enough curses out there upon people and burcaucrats to make the countryside tremble.

What harm could come from trying? She knew the rituals and incantations. The elders brought her up as a hedge witch from a young age, and after some deliberations the matter was settled. She was desperate. She would procure the items she needed to perform the ritual tomorrow night under the Strawberry Moon.

The grotesque didn't disturb her dreams again that evening and she slept peacefully. She considered this a good omen and would set about gathering the items she would need for the ritual after she broke fast with some eggs, and a little bit of the bone broth she had left over. She would need her energy.

The day flew by quickly. The last and most important item she needed for the ritual trailed behind her, tugging on the leash, a swathe of duct tape wrapped around its mouth to keep it from squealing. She tied the baby lamb to the caravan's post, and sat down on the steps for a breather. She had a lot to do before tonight's ritual.

First, she made herself eat some chicken and salad from her vegetable garden, even if she wasn't really hungry. Then she laid out the items for the ritual on the blanket she spread out onto the grass, and inventoried the items three times. And once she was satisfied everything she needed was there, she tied the four corners of the blanket together with hemp and made a silent prayer that everything would go well tonight.

Poising herself, she untied the leash from the post, and with one hand holding the leash and the other pulling the makeshift sack over her shoulder containing all the items she needed for the ritual, she climbed the embankment where she had a fire pit waiting to be lit.

Reaching the top, she tied the leash around the cattle fence post, making sure the baby lamb couldn't escape, undid her sack, and took the cauldron with her down to the River Ouse to fill it with water before lugging it back up to the fire pit.

With the fire blazing under the Strawberry Moon, she unclothed her knife, and almost faltered looking at the baby lamb pining for its mother, but the sacrifice had to be made.

She gathered up the offal and placed it in the cauldron and proceeded to spit roast the baby lamb over the fire. When cooked thoroughly she cut the baby lamb into pieces, added them to the boiling cauldron, and started the incantations, the old language rolling off her tongue naturally.

She added sage and rosemary for protection, turmeric for wits, and vervain for control, and paused to let the ingredients meld, before taking her knife and slicing her palm and letting her own blood feed the mixture.

Then she added a cold iron bracelet and stone filings she had collected from Ely Cathedral and stirred the ingredients with her knife, and when her incantations reached a crescendo and the Strawberry Moon was at its full height, she fished out the cold iron bracelet with her knife, dipped it in the Ouse water to cool, before sliding it onto her wrist, knowing instantly she was a fool for thinking the grotesque would help her. The grotesque used her body like her dead husband had. Her body was the conduit needed to restore the balance in the natural order blighted by humanity.

The Strawberry Moon turned blood red. Lightning streaked across the night sky. Dark clouds converged on Ely Cathedral, and it wasn't long before she heard the first screams, and it wasn't long after when the Cathedral Lights winked out; *why should Mother Earth suffer more?*

The new Dark Ages began.

© Stephen Port-Burke, 2024

Omerta

Angela Howard

The wind is howling across the fields. It hits the woods where I've taken shelter under an elder, although the trees here are twisting, branches waving up and down as if warning of more trouble to come. In the orchard I can see our baby apple tree swirling round and round like an un-merry-go-round faster, faster, losing its arms and limbs like a Catherine wheel. It is early evening; June, and the moon is already up. The gales are becoming more frequent in our part of the land. A few poplars near the wood's edge are starting to topple. They fall into the beeches which, incapable of holding them themselves, come careering down, the boom and crack of death throes competing with the screaming wind.

But the mistletoe clings. This is what I've come for. Caught in those fallen branches, it isn't touching the ground, which is good. But it shivers as the gusts sweep through the foliage, and so do I.

I blame it all on the moon playing tricks, disappearing, reappearing with that bright, haughty face, snatching those stringy racing clouds to lasso us, then fling us out to yet more torment. Because each month it's the same. It's not my fault, nor is it my husband's fault. Each month the same loss, the devastation, the desperation as the cycle picks up again, until the next time. The only difference is that this storm makes a noise.

The gale, here, which is gradually subsiding, is not a mere squall or a gust, but an invisible fiend, bent on rapid destruction. I lean down to pick up some mistletoe nestling in a fallen branch, but then change my mind. It's best to get some from higher up, as far above the ground as possible.

I will hang it over our door and kiss him under it; that way I'll keep him with me. He'll speak to me again, and our luck will change for the better. He won't notice it hanging there, which is just as well because he doesn't believe in these things and it might make him think I'm mad. Although he seldom notices me at all these days. I can come and go from the room countless times, or leave through the door without him ever glancing up. It's as if I'm not there, and that's what torments me. But I'm determined to win him back. Even if it's just him and me and nothing else. But he is essential for me. I think I've made my peace with the other thing. I don't want to name it, this thing that won't come.

As I hang onto the branch from where I hope to climb up and get the mistletoe, my eyes catch someone walking down the lane towards me, leaning into the wind which has rushed in once more. His jacket is flapping open, his hair is whipping his face. Taken aback, elated, I nearly let go, because it's him, my husband, and he's followed me, which means he cares. He loves me! This changes everything. Then my branch snaps and takes flight in a sudden gust, throwing me across the road in front of him and into the ditch.

This is clearly not where I belong for him, because he's coming to help me out, taking my arm, and oh, for this moment, please don't let go, never let me go. Normally, he only touches me on the fourteenth and fifteenth of my month, solely the necessary, and that's on the sofa downstairs where he now sleeps alone. I'm so grateful for the feel of his hand here on my elbow, however tight the grip as he helps me stand up. He's holding me steady. This is all I need: him holding me, loving me, never letting me go.

But he does. And I'm back in the land of doubt and despair.

How is it that just one split second, one tiny gesture, can alter your mood, your perception of things so entirely, only for it to be shattered again by another equally short and detailed gesture? I call this the pendulum effect, and it alarms me so much that I don't know what to think or believe any more.

Has he come searching for me because of the gale? Does he really care for me? At least he noticed my absence. As I say, I've been invisible for him. It needs no magic to become invisible. It only takes the one you love to never look at you, seldom touch you, and never speak to you.

When I left for this walk, he was burning those papers in the hearth. I watched him light the flames and my heart lifted, seeing his face lit up all red and glowing. But it wasn't glowing for me. Maybe he was setting fire to our life. How can I know? I've tried everything, but it seems each effort pushes him farther and makes him clam up. I've been left with no choice but to rely on magic. Mistletoe: I must find some. It will bring back what we once had, bring into the world what we so desire, help him see me, properly.

It's getting dark, and he's returning home, expecting me to follow, or so it seems. I've slipped a piece of the mistletoe into my pocket, so I don't mind being marched back as if I'm the mad one. So long as he wants me. It's turning into a beautiful night and the stars are out. I see shooting stars, too. He stops for a moment in front of me, hands in his pockets, and looks down at his feet. I walk up and see something lying there. It's glimmering.

'A fallen star,' I hear him mutter. My heart takes a leap because he has spoken at last. But then he says, 'It's the child we can't have.'

My head spins like those trees in the wind when I hear how he's put all our trouble into words, how he's finally broken his silence after such a long time. I mustn't cry. I want to hold him, to take him in my arms and promise him it will happen in the end and that I'll do whatever it takes, even though I know that's ridiculous because it's all up to the mistletoe now.

But I daren't hold him. We are too fragile. I mustn't lose him.

I look down at it. It isn't a star, but it looks like one. 'It's a glow worm,' I say, swallowing my tears, and reach down to cup it in my hands.

We pass the baby apple tree now strewn over the orchard. 'Things grow again,' he says of the destruction, gradually opening up.

I want this creature I'm holding to be a star, so I open my hands to see the glow. But caged in my palms, its light has gone out.

'Put it back in the grass,' he whispers. I quickly drop it – anything to keep him talking. I don't think it's dead because I'm sure I saw it wriggle away. That's what happens with them, doesn't it? They live on. They just don't want to stay with you.

When we arrive, I let him go inside first and wait for when his back is turned, then put my hand in my pocket for the mistletoe.

It's not there. It's not at my feet, so it hasn't fallen. I can't see it anywhere. I'm ready to run out to retrace my tracks, but of course it will have touched the ground. It's also very dark outside; the clouds have blanketed the sky. At least the moon can no longer laugh at me. Anyway, I won't leave my husband now that he's at last spoken, so I go inside.

But he, too, has vanished. He's nowhere. Everything is falling out of my grasp. I see the ashes in the fireplace: perhaps he was indeed burning our past, which I suppose is good. I clean it up, but the grey from the cinders gets under my nails and brushing them with the nailbrush and soap doesn't get it out even if I scrub and scrub. Tomorrow I'll get some more mistletoe; there's always mistletoe. Tomorrow, any day, it never really dies. He's somewhere in the house and will be wanting to set up the sofa-bed in the sitting room, so I'll go upstairs and leave him to rest because he likes to sleep early, as if sleep brings him more comfort than life.

I wipe my fingers and climb upstairs to my room to find the door ajar, which makes me start. He is lying on my bed naked. I take a quick breath, and daren't move. The moon has emerged from the clouds and lights up his body through the window so that there, laid out on the sheets, he shines like a tree brought in by the tide, smoothly sculpted by the waves and wind. I say nothing, but I'm trembling inside, repeating to myself: be careful of the pendulum, this could be a dream, this could mean nothing.

Carefully, slowly, I undress and lie beside him. He

doesn't move away. A warmth radiates from him and I sink back, sighing, waiting, hoping. Until the moon's ephemeral light reveals something on the wall above the bed.

It's my branch of mistletoe. I stiffen. How has it got there? But then his arm reaches out towards me and he starts to caress me. He's drawing me to him, his warm breath curling round my neck, gentle hands running over my shoulders, along my arms to my waist, my thighs, and now he's inside me even though this is not the fourteenth or the fifteenth of the month, and he takes me to the sky, to other lands with him where everything seems possible, after which he rests his head in the crux of my shoulder, cupping my breast in the palm of his hand.

And he speaks again, this time of the mistletoe. 'I put it there. It's good to believe. I caught it falling from your pocket. You are right.'

It is my turn to lose my words. Is this really happening? Did that moment, when he saw and caught my mistletoe, also change how he sees things? Will it stay like this? Will that pendulum stop swinging?

'But we mustn't talk about it,' he whispers. 'Mustn't look too close at things. It hurts too much. Talking frightens things away. We have to hold on, let the magic work.'

And it has. The moon, at last, gave up its tricks, and the mistletoe still hangs above our bed. I'm now in the fourth month with our star in my womb, my husband beside me, rekindling our fire.

Passing Clouds

Karin Milner

Margot ripped up the post she'd received over the past week, then tore out the pages of her diary. The pages were pretty blank anyway so nothing to lose. She couldn't come to terms with Abe smiling as he packed a suitcase and waved his passport at her.

'Japan is waiting,' he boasted.

Margot watched his ego expand to fill the room. She actually didn't say anything at all while he embraced her and got into the taxi that would take him on his dream trip to the assignment in Tokyo. Didn't notice her silence. On the silver screen, the handsome lover would pine for his woman and return from distant shores to remain by her side for eternity.

Time to move forward, she mustn't fall into the trap of searching for something that might explain what all this meant.

One Saturday afternoon, Henry, Abe's colleague called round after work.

'How about a couple of days in Southwold, the sea air will perk you up? Abe told me you have new walking boots and there are great paths to explore. Could be good.'

Henry had turned down the Tokyo opportunity and probably felt obliged to see how she was holding up. He was scruffy and well-meaning, with an enviable ability to exert a measure of control over his universe. Never got involved in anything that might pin him down or any relationship that had the aroma of romance about it.

Margot was straight with him.

'No thanks Henry, just don't have the energy for anything like that, but good of you to think up the idea.'

Renate, who she used to sit next to in Latin classes, phoned to suggest a spa break.

'It will be so good for your heart and mind, empty out all that junk. I've got a voucher, two nights for the price of one, what do you think?'

'Maybe another time, but thank you anyway,' was all she could think to say. A spa sounded so communal, the sort of place where you needed to smile at everyone unless you were asleep.

In the midst of this carnival of 'no thank yous', Margot listened to words buried deep inside her that were fighting to be heard.

If you say no often enough, people stop asking.

She dismissed the sentiment and decided on a long walk to catch the late summer sunshine and pick up bread and milk on the way home. The park was actually soothing today, sometimes it was irritating, all couples strolling by, hand in hand, or close friends immersed in stories, but not so much today. She sat on a bench and watched dogs running in circles as the sun dipped behind the trees and cooled the air before bouncing back. In previous times, this might've made her melancholic, but not today. She gazed up at the sky and palette of clouds and attempted to understand the power of summer turning into autumn, and the role of the seasons in fulfilling what the universe decreed. As the sun rose and set, the earth grew older. Its citizens had no powers, only a sea of troubles and joys, some just trying to survive, most on a quest for some measure of contentment.

A voice shattered her daydream.

'Hullo, Margot, I was going to phone you.'

Her closest friend, Betty, smiled down at her.

'Hi Betty, think I owe you a phone call, sorry I've got behind with all sorts. You know how it is.'

Betty sat down beside her in silence for a couple of minutes. She was, and always would be, someone who understood Margot and how deep the hole she could fall into unless someone cared enough to rescue her.

'Would you come round for an easy and lazy supper this Friday? Would be great to catch up in person, I get fed up with texting and want to talk to you face-to-face. Don't turn me down, Margot!'

Margot just smiled.

'Well, it's not as if I can pretend I have somewhere else to be. Go on then, what sort of time and what can I bring?'

'The right answer, around seven would be fine. I've got some alcohol-free gin so you could bring a few cans of tonic water, but not the diet stuff, tastes weird. See you Friday then.'

Margot started to feel waves of irritation at being caught out and stitched up so quickly but wouldn't be so rude as to let Betty down. An evening chatting with an old friend just had to be better than sitting at home alone. She wandered the long way home observing the different types of tree bark and change in leaf colours as summer grew old. Just like people they had their robust green days before fading into yellows and browns. She decided to buy Betty flowers in an attempt to look less grumpy.

Maybe Abe might make contact later.

That evening, Abe did indeed text a photo of the view from his office window with the simple message – 'Quite a different view eh.'

Margot was incensed at his brevity, no hint of any 'How are you?' No crumb of affection. An orange glow of anger and disappointment started to smoulder inside – how could anyone be so self-absorbed? She determined not to reply for a few days to make her level of disdain painfully clear.

Friday arrived and she walked to Betty's with a supply of tonic and a modest bouquet of late summer/early autumn.

Betty hugged her warmly and thanked her for the flowers.

'Hope you won't mind but a couple of friends have dropped round, they won't be staying long, come and meet them.'

Margot felt deflated, it was meant to be just the two of them. Nothing to be done, she was here now and so were they, probably a loved-up couple who lived in a romantic cottage overlooking the sea.

'Margot, come and meet Rose and Digby, we've known each other for ages but not as long as I've known you.'

Rose smiled and Digby uttered the words, 'Lovely to meet you, Margot.'

Chat flowed easily enough and everyone demonstrated perfect English manners. Betty and Rose disappeared into the kitchen leaving Margot to pay attention to Digby who was sitting on the sofa with a handsome dark wood cane by his side. She felt a warm and gentle vibe from him and left the many noises in her head alone as they settled into easy rather than contrived chatter.

Digby was the conversation starter.

'Always a pleasure to meet any friend of Betty's, I haven't seen her for about two months now and I'm so pleased dear Rose was able to bring me along. Good friends are a blessing, poor friendships are such a waste of time, don't you find?' Digby smiled and tapped his cane.

'Yes, you're so right, Digby, I'm about to tidy up my friendship drawer soon, needs a bit of a clear out. Anyway, have you and Rose come far this evening? I'm only a few streets away so walked here in about ten minutes.'

Before Digby could respond Rose came back into the room. 'I'll pick you up in an hour, Digby, that okay?'

'Rose, you're far too kind, if you're sure, that would be delightful.'

Margot wondered what the deal was but knew it would be rude to ask. Digby didn't feel the need to explain either, so Margot started to dream up the possibilities. Perhaps they weren't a couple, or had just called in to say hullo on their way somewhere, maybe Digby was more Betty's friend and Rose was just tagging along.

'A rose by any other name would still smell as sweet.'

Or maybe Digby was recovering from surgery and wasn't supposed to be charging around… She hoped to find out more.

Margot smiled and noticed that Digby was always smiling in much the same way a professional dancer would. He seemed so easy to be with.

'Isn't it wonderful to be out in the evening? I don't get out that much these days. How about you, Margot, do you live in a social whirl that takes you to all sorts of delights or prefer to be in a comfortable chair with a good book?'

'I'm so dreadfully boring, Digby, and haven't had an invitation to anything social for months. All my own fault, I'm lazy about keeping in touch.'

'I can hear a weariness in your voice, my dear. Don't let it worry you, my dear Margot, it's not here to stay, just a cloud passing through. There are times for feasting and dancing and times to be still and listen to the little voice inside.'

Margot felt as if her desolation was on show and attempted to hide it somewhere. 'Mm, yes, maybe you are right. You're a very perceptive man. Shall I get us some fresh drinks? Are you having the alcohol-free gin and tonic like me?'

Digby chuckled. 'Oh dear, I didn't realise I'd been conned into that. I'd love another if you'll join me. Think I can just about tolerate an alcohol-free drink as long as it's not too often.'

Margot felt a lighter sensation somewhere deep inside, a little water dampening the smouldering. Perhaps wisdom came from other people rather than books... She didn't need to wonder about Digby any more, he was funny and interesting, surely it was irrelevant to wonder who he was and why he was here. Perhaps he was wondering who the heck she was too, or simply took pleasure in the people who crossed his path.

She handed Digby a drink and sat down beside him.

'Thank you very much, Margot. Now where were we? I hate talking about politics, it's so boring. What are your views on the theatre? You know, it's an absolute passion of mine. Do you know I went to a fabulous music recital at the West Road Concert Hall last month, Elgar and Brahms, really delightful, though I do love a great big fat musical, especially if it's loud and full of life!'

He laughed at his own words in a way that Margot found quite joyous.

'I'm not really a concert goer as I haven't a clue about what's good or what's going to be heavy-going. Someone at a piano just reminds me of music lessons at school, not something you could feel sentimental about. Yes, an evening at the theatre can be great fun, can't quite remember what I saw, it was a few months ago now – ah yes, a musical built around the life of Carole King – quite a sad story really, but she wrote such wonderful and melodic tunes, I was singing them for a week afterwards.'

'Ha ha, that's excellent, I do just the same thing, the latest noise I make comes from *West Side Story*, enormous songs that shake you right up, not sure how my neighbours feel about that. They're probably fearful of what I'm going to see next! Are you sure this gin is alcohol-free, I'm feeling quite merry. Rose will think I've been up to tricks.'

Margot was feeling merry with laughter and inspired by Digby's exuberant company. What a good idea to go out for the evening, she must think about meeting more people and finding new horizons.

Betty and Rose returned, Digby took this as his cue to lean on his cane and get up from the sofa.

He struggled a little but refused assistance. 'I'm fine ladies, honestly. Oh my dear Margot, it appears I'm being collected and I haven't finished my repertoire of theatre stories yet and I've got so many! I'll have to keep them under my hat for another time. Wait till I tell you my favourite about Nigel Havers falling off the stage at the Arts Theatre! Anyway, when it's time to go, it's time to go. Lovely to see you Betty, thank you for the drinks and introducing me to the delightful Margot.'

He embraced Margot in a gentle way.

'It's been such good fun meeting you, let's do it again sometime, I think we could find so much to talk about. Keep smiling, my dear, and trust me about the passing clouds, just be ready for the new horizon, it won't be far behind.'

Margot clutched his hand and kissed his cheek. 'Hope to see you at the theatre one day.'

The visitors left and Margot watched as Rose helped Digby into the car, a distinct air of frailty surrounded him. His departure made the house feel empty.

'Betty, tell me about Digby, he's such an interesting man.'

'He's a card, isn't he! He was a friend of my parents to start with, one of those people you meet and you know that you'll always want to have in your life. He was a passionate archaeologist for many years, frequently out of the country on some dig discovering hidden treasures from the ancient world. A couple of years ago, he had a fall when rocks started collapsing at a site in Egypt and, tragically, he lost his sight. Rose is his carer and she brings him here for a visit every now and then, he loves people and is a great conversationalist. I never turn them away, life is difficult enough.'

Margot fell silent for a few moments. Should she be annoyed that he didn't declare his blindness when they were introduced, or was he wise to withhold this for fear of being treated differently?

Abe sent another message – 'You're quiet, everything okay?'

She ignored it.

Betty appeared with bread, salad and chicken. 'Let's eat outside, Margot, while it's warm enough.'

'Why not, such a lovely clear evening.'

'So, Margot, how are things?'

Points of Darkness

Tim Lagé-Hayes

In the mid-nineties, my wife and I bought a special house, a detached Victorian Gentleman's residence, on two acres of land on a steep hillside in North Devon. It was located on the east side of a valley which sheltered the village of Weare Gifford just south of Bideford. Down the middle of the valley ran the river Torridge. The property was named Weare House, denoting some meaningful status in the village in years gone by. Weare House had two not-insignificant claims to fame. First was to use its location and setting to impress on the one hand, my family back in the Southeast and, on the other, any avid readers of the author Henry Williamson we happened to meet because our new home overlooked the river and a stone bridge in the valley of Tarka the Otter. Second, a neat factoid. My dear wife had been delivered into this world by her mother's then General Practitioner, who, at the time, was the proud occupant of the very same Weare House.

It took some weeks, and then more, to refurbish and redecorate, including fitting an expensive period marble fireplace and having a builder cut cavities into the three-foot stone dividing wall separating the two main bedrooms at the front of the house to make wardrobes. We also instructed the builder to remove the thick dividing wall between the two reception rooms on the ground floor, giving us a splendid spacious room with a 180° visibility of our garden and the valley beyond.

We moved down to Devon from our house in Hertfordshire to supervise the building works, during which time we stayed in a small cottage on the hill in the village of Appledore. We had stayed there several times over the previous two years. We had not been married for long; our cottage was a sort of love nest that we visited for weekends away from the hustle and bustle of the Southeast. The cottage came with panoramic views over the Torridge Estuary and the nuisance of having to park our car a hundred yards away down the hill accessed by a rough path.

One of the things my wife and I had in common was that we both came from dysfunctional childhoods followed by broken marriages. The latter was not an unusual state of being in those days when, twenty years earlier, young men were still obliged to wed the girl for the sake of her unborn child, and many young ladies hadn't the wisdom or confidence to say 'no' when propositioned by a persistent suitor.

From the outset, our relationship blossomed because of our ability to have deep and, as we both felt, meaningful conversations about life, the universe, and everything. Well, not like that. We had both arrived on the cusp of middle age, having hit a brick wall. As I once heard a man say, 'If you want to know what God's will is for you when you hit a brick wall, turn left.' Speaking for myself, the God of my childhood had been banished from my life many years ago, beaten out of me at boarding school by a

Benedictine monk.

For those asking the question, 'What is Darkness?' one answer can be derived from the answer to an old Christmas cracker joke, which reads, 'Where was Moses when the lights went out?'

But, if you have ever been in your mind to somewhere called 'the jumping off place,' then you would know that darkness is not a result of turning off a light, nor is it a deep space black hole where the immense gravitational forces prevent even light from escaping. If we think in spiritual terms, it is, I suggest, a state of mind where the perception of one's future life is blotted and darkened out altogether. It is a state of mind where one can no longer live with something or someone or some habit, nor can one live without he or she or it. It is a moment of knowledge when the pain of living afflicted by that particular existence or behaviour becomes more significant than the projected pain of living without it.

In my life, just once, I was gifted with that left turn. I had been consulting at a firm down in the port of Dover. I was staying away for the week in a hotel. It was a Friday evening, in a dark and cold early January 1985. Before I started driving home, I stopped at the petrol station, which in those days stood just inside the entrance to the main ferry port. I had just finished filling my car when a young woman approached me.

'Excuse me, sir,' she spoke with a French accent, 'do you have a pound you can give me, please?'

When I asked for what purpose, she told me she had lost her purse with her tickets inside and could not return home. I asked her how much she needed and was told a figure of thirty pounds, which I happened to be carrying. I gave her the money and wished her well.

Before she walked away, her last words were, 'May

God reward you.'

Now, I have to say that soon after I drove off, I examined my conscience and concluded that my motive had been to help that person avoid further begging. I may have completely misread the situation, but so what? As I drove home for the next few hours, her parting words echoed around my mind. I was very down on luck and desperately needed a helping hand. Those parting words came back to me time after time over the long weekend.

On Monday, I was back at my office and to my usual way of life. Last week was forgotten. That was the day I realised I had hit a brick wall. I arrived back home late. The household had already gone to bed. I stood in my kitchen, turned to the ceiling, and whispered to the God of my childhood. I sheepishly apologised for being out of contact for so long and said I needed help. No flash, bang. Nothing happened, but it had.

The next day, I awoke to find I had been given one of the greatest gifts of all: willingness. Willingness to turn left. Willingness to reach out for help, which was willingly given to me in bucketloads. Ahead of me was the door to a spiritual journey if I chose to take it. There have been many more brick walls when I have been unsure of the 'right thing' to do. I have learned to listen to that voice within me. I was given a book where I read, 'See that your relationship with Him is right, and great things will come to pass for you and countless others.' Willingness to close and open the doors of life is the key.

Another kind of darkness was brought to public attention by the renowned American psychiatrist M. Scott Peck. He was best known for his book *The Road Less Travelled*, which was first published in 1978 and, in those days, to be found on mini bookshelves in all beautiful people's cloakrooms. After handling several alarming cases of patients whom he found particularly resistant to any form of help, Scott Peck authored a book about this, which he called *People of the Lie: The Hope for Healing Human Evil.* He had come to class those patients as exhibiting an extreme type of self-righteousness, naming it akin to malignant narcissism.

The person who first lent me the book, *People of the Lie*, did so cautiously: 'Read with care,' I was told. It is a very dark and disturbing book. One of the early stories in the book is of a poor, churchgoing American family. They had two sons. One Christmas, they gave their eldest son a gun as a present. In the months which followed, that son was one day found dead, having shot himself. The family grieved this significant loss of life.

About a year later, the parents came to Scott Peck seeking advice concerning their younger son. He had previously had an excellent academic record, but although it had been a year since his elder brother had died, his work had started going downhill to such an extent that the school had advised his parents to seek help. Interviews with the boy were to no avail, and after a time when Scott Peck thought he could take the case no further, he felt that the problem must be related to the parents. He decided to recommend that the boy should go to stay with a distant aunt. The boy's behavioural condition stabilised, and soon after moving, he started improving. Curious about this, Scott Peck re-interviewed the boy away from his parents and learned the root cause of his problems. At the Christmas following his brother's death, the boy was given his dead brother's gun. He had seen it as a message from his parents to go and kill himself, as his brother had done.

Scott Peck returned to see the parents, who were shocked at the suggestion that they could have done anything wrong, saying they were a low-income family who could not afford such fine presents. They could see nothing wrong with giving this fine present to their second son and refused further help.

Scott Peck described this behaviour in his book as 'subtle scapegoating,' and I could understand exactly what he meant. Parental messaging can, without intention on the part of the parent, be very damaging. A simple example in my childhood was meeting with my father at nine as he read my primary school report with end-of-term exam results. Overall, first in class. I got top scores in six of nine subjects and second in class for the remainder.

Teachers left small comments; most read, 'Well done!' and, 'Good work!' I cannot remember the subject my father chose to focus on, but it was something like history, where I was first in class. The teacher had written, 'Could do better if he tried harder.' Looking back, the teacher must have considered that I could achieve higher markings. The hidden message I heard from my father, who had drawn my attention to this rather than the other well-earned comments, was that I was not good enough for him.

The issue this raised for me is that however well-meaning my father was in his communication, how I had received and processed his choice of words was the polar opposite of what was intended.

Twelve years ago, I started another journey when one of my children was falling behind in his speech. I took him to the doctor, who asked him, 'So, what school are you at?' my son answered correctly. The next question came. 'Where are you going next?'

To this, my son answered, 'North, South, East? I don't know.' The GP suggested an educational psychologist would assist, telling me I would not get an appointment for at least a year. I called his school and repeated what had happened at the GP. 'Oh!' she said, 'He is taking things "literally". That is a trait of autism, but I can tell you he is not autistic.'

Three months later, my son was diagnosed with Asperger's syndrome, a type of autism spectrum disorder (ASD). A deep dive on the internet reveals a mine of information on the subject, including self-test questionnaires which indicate the likelihood of being 'on the spectrum.' Curious about myself, I did not have to try harder on this simple fifty-question test, scoring forty-five out of fifty positive markers.

A year later, I, too, was diagnosed with Asperger's. It wasn't a badge, but it explained my life's trajectory. Asperger's Syndrome had only been formally described and categorised as a neurodivergent condition in the years 1993 to 1995, and autism spectrum disorders in 2005 to 2006. Like Moses, when the light went out, I had grown up and lived sixty years of my life entirely in the dark. Thousands of people of my age remain undiagnosed. Some refer to us as 'the lost generation'.

I have had a rollercoaster relationship with my parents and siblings. My behaviour and, indeed, my life decisions have not been without negative comments. So, more recently, I started labelling myself as the 'black sheep' of the family. My father kept laying into me until the day he died. He opposed my choice of career, which was to be self-employed. On one occasion, he told me my problem was that I did not 'conform'. He told me about a cousin of mine and her husband who also did not 'conform', but that after many years, my cousin's husband got himself a 'proper job', which he told me I ought to do.

Talking about sheep brings me back to Weare House – which, by the way, the purchase of which was yet another of my father's criticisms. 'Why, on earth, do you need to buy that house with all its large garden? You will never be able to keep it up,' he told me.

The building works and decoration were finally completed. Funnily enough, my wife and I were so accustomed to living in the cottage that we struggled to recall why we bought Weare House in the first place. But the day came when we did move in. We took actual ownership, walking around the garden and woods on the hillside above the house. We lit an open log fire, we cooked our first meal, and as we sat in our dining room late in the afternoon, we were pleasantly surprised when the muntjacs came down from the woods onto the lawn just outside the casement doors.

Finally, after a long day, we retired to our bedroom. We turned out our bedside lights, and… quite unexpectedly… it was dark – completely black, dark, nothingness. I got up to look outside through the window; no lights could be seen anywhere. There was no moon, no stars; it had clouded over. The faint glow of distant streetlights was missing. And it was dead silent. There were no cars about, even on the main road along the other side of the valley. The silence somehow accentuated the darkness.

The sound of sheep bleating is a common experience for country folk – no need for an alarm clock. Not long after dawn, the sheep and their newborn lambs grazing in the field over the other side of the river woke us. In the days to come, I learned much about life by studying the sheep. Unlike humans, these creatures could live from one end to the other without going to school or holding down a job to feed their family. I even saw the occasional black sheep and was comforted, finally knowing I was not alone.

The Bone Cleaners

Alice Hughes

* 2nd place *

Evie was sitting on a cushion at the coffee table, drawing a shiny black Bone Cleaner beetle. In the *The Art of Taxidermy* book, his magnified oval body was covered in tiny yellow hairs. His antennae were clubbed like black lavender at the tips. The beetles were no bigger in real life than her middle fingernail, but could crawl lightning-fast and eat the flesh from a deer skull in a day. Her mother Sara had bought a colony of them to clean bones after skinning animals. For several months they'd been living in the locked side-room of her studio, which was off limits.

The princess song from Rose's handheld game console filled the living room. *"To be a princess is to always look your best."* It grew louder. *"To be a princess is to never get to rest."* Evie pushed hard on the sketchpad with her pencil, snapping the lead.

'Ro-Ro, turn it down!' She threw the lead at Rose, who was curled in the armchair, wearing her red cape. Evie was twelve, exactly twice the age of her sister, and didn't like dressing up. She preferred her black dungarees.

'If you don't like my princess, go to your room,' Rose said.

Last summer was the best ever. Their grandma had been alive then and Rose stayed with her, while Evie was trusted to be Sara's mole school assistant. Aside from selling work to museums and collectors, teaching taxidermy was a way to earn money. Sometimes, the students bought Sara's work. Evie became skilful at moles. The students cheered at how quickly her fingers turned the skin inside out. They'd gasped when she demonstrated how to remove the flesh from tricky bones.

Now, she missed spending time with Sara who needed to be alone in her studio preparing for her debut *Speaking Bones* exhibition. It was her big break to show the world why taxidermists should be recognised as artists. There was no time to teach Evie skeleton preparation. It was her first time working with the Bone Cleaner beetles. She had to be careful. 'It would be a disaster if they escaped. They eat everything. And skull and bone preparation is more difficult than usual taxidermy. Once the beetles have eaten the flesh, every bone has to be rearranged into skeletons. I've spent years learning the animals' anatomies,' she'd said. There was no time to forage for mushrooms either. Evie withdrew into her shell. She put up with Rose.

That evening, Sara had another meeting with the curator of the *Speaking Bones* exhibition. She unearthed a long-sleeved black dress with a white collar that Evie had never seen. She gave her and Rose a rare lipstick kiss goodbye on her way out. It was strange to see her dressed up and not in her Pink Floyd hoodie.

Evie tried to sit still on the chaise longue. She was reading *The Adventures of Huckleberry Finn*. Dermestidae. Dermestidae. Dermestidae. The Bone Cleaners' proper name was stuck in her head. Scribbled in the margins of the book. It meant *to consume skin.*

'Ro-Ro,' she shouted, dropping the book on the floor. 'Come quick, we're going on an adventure.'

The keys were in Sara's bedroom beneath her giant knickers and rubbery period cups. Evie was good at secret missions. They had to be back in the house before 9.00 p.m. when Sara sometimes phoned. She set a timer on her wristwatch.

'What adventure?' Rose asked.

'We're going to see the Bone Cleaners. Just one look – see, then we'll get ready for bed.'

They put their boots on by the back door. She tied Rose's cape to stop it dragging in the dirt. They squelched into the dark garden towards the studio. Evie zipped up her raincoat. Her pulse throbbed. She caught spiderwebs strung across the grass with her torchlight. Rose slid on mud and grabbed her hand.

'The moon is missing,' she whispered, tightening her grip.

Evie ignored this ridiculous observation, dragging her through the wind.

'Why is the moon missing, Evie? I'm scared.'

'Remember what I said about being brave? You have to be, or you'll end up boring. Fight or flight?'

'Fight.' She raised her fist, smudged by dark.

The edges of the rectangular white studio were sharp. Moths were stuck to the sliding glass door, hankering for the orange glow of heat lamps inside. The beetles needed warmth to live. Evie unlocked and slid the door open.

'Will the Bone Cleaners eat us?' Rose asked, as they took off their boots.

'No. They don't like the taste of us,' Evie said.

There were no windows to spy through into the locked side-room where the beetles lived. When they went inside, it was filled with heat lamps like the main room and felt cosy, except for the death-stench. They pinched their noses. Evie switched on the light and lifted the cloth from the centre table. A muntjac deer tilted his antlers to greet them, his skeleton held up by poles. On the side-table, three rabbit skeletons crouched under cloth, their thumps preserved in hind leg bones. She removed the cloth, ran her fingers along the smallest rabbit's spine and let Rose have a turn.

Rose giggled at the nobbles. 'Hey, Mr Thump, that tickles.'

Evie covered the rabbits up. On the opposite side of the room, she spotted the beetles' home. It was a large container which looked like an old freezer. The heavy lid was hard to lift. She held it open with a shaky hand and bent her head for a look, gagging at the whiff of droppings and uneaten flesh. Thousands of shiny reddish-brown larvae wriggled in the wood shavings. They had a yellow central line on their bodies and were covered in spiky hairs. Most kept to the edges on Styrofoam bedding, some were brave enough to venture into the middle. Every few seconds, a black adult beetle crawled fast through the larvae.

Rose was calmer now, humming the princess song. 'Friendly babas. I'm going to make you wriggle dance,' she declared, leaning over the container. She poked her finger deep into the larvae. 'Ewwwwwwwww. Sticky wrigglers,' she giggled.

Something flew into Rose's face. She screamed and pulled her finger out, waving her arms. Evie jumped forward and two adult beetles opened their wings and shot out in opposite directions. How could they fly? *The Art of*

Taxidermy book hadn't warned her. One by one more beetles twitched awake, splitting their wings. They flew out at dizzy angles quicker than Evie could think. After a few seconds, she grabbed a roll of newspaper and tried to squish them in the air. At least thirty were zig zagging through the side-room door into the main studio.

'The lid!' Rose cried.

Evie slammed the lid shut.

'Where did they fly, Rose?'

'I don't know.'

She grabbed Rose's arm, dragged her out and bolted the side-room. The main studio door was partly open.

'Why did you leave the door open, Rose?'

'I didn't! It was you.' Rose stamped her foot.

'Quick, we have to find them.'

Evie searched under the tablecloth on the work table in the centre of the room. She inspected the stacked newspaper at one end. Checked the shelves at the back. Rummaged in boxes of bottles, wood wool, moss, borax powder and clay. Rose whimpered, peeking inside the tool draws.

'They're too good at hiding places,' she whined.

Evie sighed. 'They must have escaped into the garden.'

The timer on her wristwatch went off. She made sure everything was put back in place, then locked the studio door. Rose squealed at the crack of a twig. Evie squeezed her hand. Slimy grass was stuck to the soles of their boots. They wiped them on the scraper mat by the back door. They hurried inside and hugged each other, waiting for the phone to ring. It didn't. No missed calls.

Upstairs, Evie made Rose promise she wouldn't tell. Rose held her pinky promise finger to the bathroom mirror as Evie scrubbed a flannel over her face. She head-butted her chest and started to cry.

It was a month since the Bone Cleaners had broken free. Sara had finished preparing her works for the *Speaking Bones* exhibition, but was still busy at the gallery or working on her laptop most nights. While Sara was busy, Evie's job, when she wasn't at school, was to clean the taxidermy collection in the house. Over the last week, she had started to find piles of sawdust. Shed larvae skins that looked like Rice Krispies. Dark brown stringy hairs which she learned were beetle poo. Tracks made in the fur of Todd Fox. Even Ratty in his glass dome. The Bone Cleaner colony was now gone from Sara's studio, but the escapees must have made their way into the house.

The Art of Taxidermy book said the female Bone Cleaners laid eggs in the crevices of what they were feeding on. From the moment a larvae hatched, they ate for the rest of their life, which could be months long. Every night that week, she hugged herself in her bed. She cried under her duvet. Rose had kept her secret so far and didn't know the beetles were in the house. Sara had been too busy to notice the signs. Evie was the only one who heard them crying in pain.

Whenever Sara was out late, Evie opened the windows. She sprayed insecticide around the house, but couldn't use too much. She hoovered everything. Washed the cushions and blankets. Tumble dried and put them back before Sara got home. It was useless. The only real solution was to freeze the taxidermy collection, which was impossible to do in secret.

That Sunday, Evie found Sara sitting at the kitchen table.

'Good morning, Evie.' Sara smiled, glancing up at her. 'Do you want to have a peek at my exhibition before you get to see it?'

'Yes please.' Evie pulled a chair next to her.

Sara found the photo album on her camera. In the first photo, red plastic bags were caught like a heart in the ribcage of the muntjac deer.

'Which would decompose fastest?' Sara asked.

'The deer bones?'

'Correct. Plastic bags can take up to 10,000 years. Bones usually take a decade.'

The next photo was the rabbit skeletons hopping along the gallery floor, leaving a trail of black footprints. 'They have secret spoors.' Sara stood up. 'Ways of seeing and feeling and speaking that we cannot know. I better get back to work.'

Rose clacked hurriedly into the kitchen wearing her heeled jelly shoes. 'Evie, look,' she held out her palm to show a clump of Todd Fox's auburn bushy tail. Evie glanced quickly at Sara, who was lacing up her boots by the back door. She jumped from her chair and dragged Rose with a hand over her mouth into the living room, until she heard the back door close.

'I can't breathe!' Rose yelled.

'Remember your promise about the Bone Cleaners?' Evie warned. 'If you tell Mum about this, they'll eat you in your dreams.'

The next day, while Sara was in her studio, Rose's questions kept coming. 'Will they eat me tonight?' 'Can they hear my princess song?' 'Who would win in a fight, a Bone Cleaner or a spider?'

That night, they ate dinner together. Sara slopped

vegetarian curry on their plates and told Rose to turn her game sound down. She went back to reading her speech notes for the preview evening of the exhibition.

'Mum?' Evie tried to get her attention. She had to tell her.

'Just finish your dinner,' Sara didn't look up. 'No time. Not tonight. I've got to get ready.'

Sara put on a new white dress for the preview. Silky slim with a slit to one side. Twinkling tummy belt. Hair pinned back, showing her elf ears. She wore a necklace of mouse skulls.

'A true princess,' Rose neighed around her.

Evie woke to the whistle of wood pigeons. She wondered how the preview evening had gone, but daren't wake Sara up.

She tiptoed down the stairs. The kitchen door was open.

Sara was pacing around. Why was she still awake in her white dress? *Panthera uncia.* An angry snow leopard. Her half-eaten swan in tatters on the table. Swanhilde was no longer fluffy and majestic, but covered in bald patches. She was detached from her wooden mount.

Sara sobbed and picked her swan up. 'Look at Swanhilde. My favourite. I trusted–' Her snivels cut her words short.

Evie had caught Sara crying a few times while spying, but not like this. She flinched with each of Sara's wounded looks past her. A sick bubble rose in her throat. Her tears spurted out. 'I'm sorry, Mum. I-I didn't mean it. I love them too.'

'And this is how you show it?' Sara looked at Swanhilde madly, flailing her scrappy neck. She whined, scrunching her face at the feathers on the floor.

'I tried to tell you. I'm so sorry, Mum.' Evie stepped closer. 'Can't we fix them?'

'No. Everything's ruined,' Sara backed away, cradling her swan. 'I thought you understood what they mean to me. I thought I could trust you.'

Autumn sun beamed through the studio door and danced on Sara's bare shoulders. She kept stepping back and instructing Evie on how to get Mr Darcy's facial expression like the photo pinned to the easel in front of them. He was a snarly tabby cat that belonged to their neighbour Mrs Price. As part of the deal for his resurrection, Mrs Price took care of Rose on weekends.

'Brush his fur in the direction of his brow. That's it,' Sara said.

'His glass eye's all dirty,' Evie pointed, biting her lip.

'It's just caulk. Use acetone on your toothbrush. It will crumble off.'

'I like this part better than when we cut him in half.'

Sara laughed. She seemed happier now her new works were selling better after the *Speaking Bones* exhibition. 'He's nearly complete. Let's go on a mushroom forage as a reward.'

Evie raced ahead in the woods, following an invisible map of spores through the oak trees. She remembered the ache their legs had felt after checking and cleaning every specimen, salvaging only a few items from the collection. Just before Sara burned the remains, Evie had seen the box of her infested friends by the back door. She lifted a pile of wood wool to find Todd Fox's sunken face and hollow eyes: a Halloween mask drowning in a jumble of fur, feathers, larvae skins, glass eyes, clay heads and mounts. That night, Sara had sat in the garden, staring at the fire until it dwindled into embers.

'Want to nibble a velvet shank?' Sara asked, catching up with a basket full of sticky orange mushroom caps. Evie took one and savoured its nutty taste.

The Coming of Cholera

Lorraine Morley

* 3rd place *

My grandmother had the gift of second sight, at least that is what she always told us. Sometimes the things she told us *would* happen, *did* happen, but then they were something usually so obvious, so predictable, that her prophetic claims seemed hardly like a feat of clairvoyance.

One day, she woke up and couldn't see. We took her to every doctor in the district all of whom could find no physical affliction that would account for the loss of her sight. My grandma, lying in her bed, quiet and resigned, told us she had *not* lost her sight, she could see perfectly well. The problem was that her visions of the future showed only darkness.

After a few weeks and with no sign that my grandmother was improving, we had given up on the doctors and turned to the priests. And after the priests we turned to the shamans and after the shamans, the witch doctors. I travelled far and wide to discover a cure, but no one could find the root of my grandmother's plight. She lay in bed day after day, week after week, her slight form almost invisible among the jumble of sheets. I sat with her whenever I could, reading to her, encouraging her to eat, guiding her hand to the spoon and then the spoon to her mouth. No more than a few drops of soup passed her lips. From time to time, a tear would mark a trail from the edge of her eye, along the soft down crinkle of her cheek and drop silently onto her pillow. She did not talk much. Just from time to time, she would murmur, 'It's coming.'

We were at a loss to understand what trouble might be brewing. The long and wide horizons of our land were clear so it couldn't be a storm, and our relations with other tribal groups around us, for once, were settled and calm.

'What can it be?' I asked, crouching by her bedside, her soft, small hand held gently in mine.

From time to time, her grasp would tighten with a strength that surprised me and, turning her head, she would look at me with those blank eyes, looking into a future I couldn't see. 'Leave, you must leave.'

I took this message back to the elder circle who listened to me each time with surprising patience. They had a lot of respect for my grandmother. But even for those used to the interpretation and conveying of messages through symbols and dreams, more persuasion was needed.

'Your grandmother is old. Perhaps she hovers somewhere in the twilight between the living and the dead. We cannot move our village, the families, the livestock, without being more certain. We are settled here. This place gives us everything we need – pasture, shelter, water. We honour your grandmother, we love your grandmother, but on this one thing she says, we cannot place all our trust.'

That summer, through our toil and hard work, we watched our crops flourish, our livestock fatten, and our children grow. I still sat with my grandmother every day, on a small hard stool I had crafted myself, and I prayed for her recovery. She lay on her back in the narrow bed, more like a child than a woman, staring up at the ceiling and now and then she would raise her arms as if she was trying to push something away.

'Please,' she said into the shadows, 'please don't take them,' and then she would turn her face towards me and open her barren eyes wide, and in that moment, I too felt I could see and feel the darkness.

One evening, quite late, after I had spent the evening with my friends and neighbours around the fire, discussing the bounty that the harvest had given us, laughing with each other about the matters of the day, chatting about our families, about our dreams of the future, I had a sudden urge to see my grandmother. Stepping out of the glow of the fire and, even though the night was warm, I shivered a little. I entered my grandmother's small shack and, feeling around for the lantern I knew was there, lit it with a taper I had carried with me. Setting it down by her bed, I took my customary seat by her side, not expecting her to be awake but wanting to be with her, all the same. As I sat there, I saw her hand emerge from the light cotton cover and feel for mine.

She turned her head to me and said, 'It's here.'

They were the last words she uttered.

From a distance we watched the steady decimation of villages in our neighbourhood and the wave of grief and despair that accompanied it. We thought, by some miracle, by some amazing stroke of luck, that it had passed us by. As we watched it, we felt slightly remote. And blessed and grateful.

As it seemed the spread of the disease was slowing, was drifting off away from the coast and towards the inner lands, we held a celebration in honour of my grandmother and in the relief that she had been wrong. But the disease duped us and came anyway, like a thief in the night, and took our loved ones, our elders, our neighbours. But mostly, it took our children. The village has fallen silent, devoid of their patter and the noise of their laughter.

At first, we got the mildest of symptoms, a little loosening of the bowels, an elevated temperature. Then it came with a force and ferocity that stripped from us even our most basic faculties and left us entirely unable to cope with the next onslaught; the vomiting, the hallucinations conjured up by extreme dehydration, the shock to the body of the rampant infection and then, not long before death, there came the darkness.

Twenty-four hours is all it took and that is not enough time to say one's goodbyes. To give time for the apologies, the chance to reflect on the imprint of one's life, for the chance to grieve in private. There was no peace to be had, no gentle silence as one slipped away.

A close community, living side by side, is something we thought made us stronger, but it became the lightning rod by which the disease travelled. The norms and habits of our community; the touching, the sharing, the embracing, was instead our undoing.

We never came to know the origin of that first infection. It could have been one of the boats or canoes which stopped briefly at the mooring point on the river near our village. We watched as the fishermen emptied their rubbish and effluent into the rank river water already depleted by a late drought and, with levels so low, there formed a slew of rancid mud along the river's edge. Or it could have been someone we knew: a friend, a neighbour, a passive carrier unaware of the danger they were bringing home. It could have been me, reaching out everywhere I could to find a cure for my grandmother's blindness. I am not sure it matters now.

The Darkness

Kathy English

One of the few advantages of being a care-leaver is that you get priority for university housing. So I am all fixed up with a nice studio for my second year while my friends are still scrambling to find anything affordable on the private market.

I can't move in until September, but that's okay; I'm off to the Mendips for the summer. The job in Spooky Hole sounds ideal: £350 a week with free board and lodging.

'But what if you don't like it? Where will you go?' Emma asks.

My reply: 'Then I don't like it,' puzzles her; with her privileged background, Emma cannot conceive of sticking at something unpleasant, while a lifetime in care has made me an old hand at it. Most recently, I tolerated two years being fostered by Roger and Sylvia, even though he was way too handsy, and she was only sober when my social worker visited, because I could not risk being moved away from my school while I was studying for A Levels. So I bought a bolt for my bedroom door, wore headphones during their screaming rows, and kept working. After that, I know I can stomach ten weeks at Spooky Hole, whatever it is like.

After a couple of days, I WhatsApp Emma to reassure her that everything is fine. In fact, it's rather pleasant. We are staying in Spooky Hall, a sixteenth century farmhouse with the owners of the Hole; farmer Eric, his wife Alison and her mother Elsie.

There are amazing views from my attic bedroom and, as the other girl has failed to materialise, I have it to myself. Spooky Hole itself is breath-taking; it's a vast underground cavern full of stalagmites and stalactites, with gushing undergrounds streams and stone-age cave paintings on the wall; I have never seen anything like it.

The other seasonal workers, the boys as Alison calls them, are all from the same Oxford College and react as though they've never heard of Midlands Uni. They've been here for a couple of weeks, and take it in turns to supervise the car park and take the customers on a tour of the caves. I shall be taking over from Alison in the ticket office. It looks easy enough.

Elsie looks after the house and cooks us lovely meals. She is clearly lonely; she moved here for company after she was widowed to find that Eric and Alison work very long hours and that living on a remote farm is not conducive to an active social life. She is so pleased to have my company in the evenings that I already know most of the family history.

Eric and Alison bought the farm shortly after they married and are sheep famers. Spooky Hole was closed to the public for fifty years until Alison inherited some money and spent it on creating the car park, building a toilet block, re-wiring the caves and replacing the ancient boardwalks so that they could re-open and 'diversify away from sheep'. The works were far more expensive than anticipated so they are now burdened with a bank loan, and are desperate to make a success of this first season.

Today is my first day off. I sleep until eleven! It could be because I am so often woken in the night; Alison says the bizarre noises are made by foxes, but they don't make those sounds in the city.

The work is far more tiring than I expected. We are still a member of staff short, so I am trying to sell ice-creams as well as tickets.

And a lot of the public don't seem able to read. The notice board is clear enough; under-fives free, under-eighteens £5, adults £10, no concessions, no prams, buggies or dogs (except guide dogs), yet people are continually asking for information that's in front of their eyes. And they are so argumentative. Yesterday, I had a man complaining that by refusing to admit his dog, we were discriminating against him for not being blind. I ask you.

When I am dressed, I walked the mile into the village and visit the pub for the first time. The boys go most evenings, but I have been staying home; I can't afford to drink away my earnings.

As I sip my cider, I hear Spooky Hole mentioned.

'I told them straight,' a buxom woman at the bar says to a man in an ancient tweed jacket, 'I'd rather lose my Universal Credit than work there.'

I think they may have noticed me looking at them, for she speaks more quietly after that. I hear her say, 'the darkness' a couple of times so assume she has nyctophobia (meaning fear of the dark – I googled it). It is incredibly dark in the caverns; they turn the lights off on every tour to impress the punters and I have never seen blackness like it. I wonder if I should have told her that the vacancy is for an ice-cream seller who need never enter the cave.

Later, I pop into the Post Office to buy a postcard for 'Gran', the nicest lady I've ever lived with.

'You'll be the lass working at Spooky Hole,' the shop assistant says as I look in amazement at the three different tractor magazines on the counter. 'Do be careful, won't you.

'Did they tell you all about the darkness? I bet they didn't,' she adds as we wait for the incredibly slow card reader to do its business. I have the impression she is going to add something, but Eric walks in and talk turns to the weather.

What is it with the locals and darkness? It's an odd thing to worry about when you live in an area without street lights.

One of the boys, Marcus, has broken his leg playing football. Alison spent six hours in A & E with him and is now fussing as though he's her son. To me, the injury means that he can't do his job and should leave, but Alison has transferred him to the ticket office (without consulting me) and put Elsie in charge of ice-cream sales, as well as the cooking.

She is decidedly miffed as she was due to visit a friend in Bath for a week; her daughter is apologetic but adamant that we are short of staff and cannot do without her. Yet, when I suggest advertising the vacancy in the Post Office, they both look at me as though I am mad.

'Local people wouldn't want to work here,' is Elsie's explanation. It makes no sense.

*

I am now the 'back person'; I walk at the rear of every tour carrying a huge flashlight, and make sure none of the group gets left behind. By the fifth tour of the day, it is mind-numbingly dull. Accompanying the groups makes me realise that a lot of the guests have questions that we cannot answer. It doesn't seem to have occurred to Alison and Eric that visitors would want information about what they are seeing; the age of the cave paintings, for example. There are some pretty negative comments about this on Trip Advisor, which is hardly helpful for a new venture.

There must have been an archaeological study at some time; surely there is more information about the cavern somewhere? When I can find nothing online, I decide to visit the local library on my day off. If I can get some information maybe they'll let me have a go at guiding.

Not knowing where to start, I ask the librarian if they have any information on Spooky Hole.

'Of course,' she says. 'Wait there.' It is a good ten minutes before she reappears. To my surprise, she is carrying an unwieldly, large, black parcel tied together with yellow ribbon. It is only as she lays it down on the desk that I understand; the front bears a peeling label: *Mendip Weekly 1973*.

'I'll have to leave you to it, there's a queue,' she says, 'but I think it was in June.' She is gone before I can ask what 'it' is.

Anyway, I begin at the 1st of June, scanning reports of gymkhanas and cricket matches, long-winded obituaries and numerous pages of wedding photographs, before finding what I am seeking. The headline leaps off the front page:

Tragedy at Spooky Hole; has the Darkness struck again?

The feature covers three whole pages and is lavishly illustrated with pictures of the inside of the cavern and Spooky Hall. The nub of the story is that the power failed during a tour of the cavern, plunging the party into darkness. As one employee had gone home earlier pleading a headache, they had been accompanied by just one member of staff, Tom. According to Tom's account, in the ensuing panic, his flashlight had been knocked off a railing into the depths below. Others said that the batteries in his light had failed.

Today, people would simply turn on their phones. Fifty years ago, they had nothing more than the odd cigarette to help them. Tom had, very sensibly, I thought, told them all to sit down and wait while he went for assistance. I don't envy him having to make his way out of the caves in the dark, but he had apparently done so reasonably quickly and returned with several torches and more helpers.

It was when the party reached safety that the trouble really began. As a routine precaution, they counted the number leaving the cave; twenty-eight adults and five children. The problem was that their records showed that twenty-nine adults had gone in.

According to the Mendip Weekly, the police, cave-divers and mountain rescue had all been searching the cavern without success. Strangely, the identity of the person they were searching for was unknown; no-one had been reported missing.

I find a separate interview with the employee who left pleading a headache, in which she claims to have had a premonition of disaster. Over the page, there is an article about 'the Darkness'. Apparently, that was the name the villagers had always given the caves. 'Spooky Hole' and 'Spooky Hall' were recent inventions, thought up by Lord

Arvon when he'd purchased the site a few years before.

'I warned him,' an unnamed local woman is quoted as saying. 'I said no good would come of opening up the darkness. It has always eaten those who dare to go inside.'

I understand now why the caves were closed fifty years ago and the locals still don't want to work there; an unexplained death in living memory is enough to put anybody off.

But when I flick to the next edition, I am surprised to discover the story is not mentioned until page five, where the headline reads:

No-one lost in the Darkness.

Apparently, after three days of the rescue services searching the cavern, Lord Arvon discovered that the number of adult tickets sold had been 28, not 29. His staff had miscounted the size of the party; no one was missing. The editorial fulminated about the careless waste of public funds and volunteers' time.

As the bus back weaves its way at scary speeds along the winding lanes, I ponder what I have discovered. It makes no sense. Closing because of a fatality would be understandable; closing because of a counting error is not. I realise, too, that I have failed to find anything on the archaeology of the caves.

'I hope you're not going to leave us,' Elsie says when I tell her what I have discovered.

'No, but I don't get it,' I reply. 'No-one died. Why are the locals so frightened?'

There is a long silence before she answers, 'Because we all thought there was a death.'

'But the ticket numbers…?'

'…Will only agree with the number on the tour if

everyone buys a ticket.'

'They think someone sneaked in?'

'No, but someone who didn't have to pay was often there.'

'Who?'

'Edwin, Lord Arvon's eldest son. He was a little, what we called, simple. He loved the caves and would often join the tours, but never bought a ticket. Tom was sure he'd been there that day and that the count of 29 was correct. And from that day onward no-one ever saw Edwin again.' She says this last part with a flourish as though this is a well-rehearsed story.

I protest that Lord Arvon would have known if his son was missing.

'There are stories that he knew only too well,' Elsie says, 'Stories that he had the body whisked out of the caves in the dead of night to cover up the death.'

'But why?'

'Some said so he could re-open the caves; it was a flourishing business and he didn't want the tragedy to kill it. Others pointed out that Bella, whose dad ran the Coach and Horses had just had a rather unexpected baby boy – she was only 15 – and people were saying it was Edwin's. And with his being the eldest son, that kid would have been the heir. Knowing Edwin, he'd have gone round with a huge smile on his face telling everyone the baby was his, so the family wanted him out of the way.'

I stare at her. 'But that suggests they murdered him? Had him murdered? That the power cut was staged?'

'That's what people said. I don't say I believe it. But they got the witnesses out of the way pretty quick. Tom was sacked and evicted from his cottage so he had to leave the village and Bella's dad suddenly got the chance of managing a much larger pub in the Yorkshire Dales. We never did see Edwin again. The family said he'd gone off travelling, but if you ask me, he didn't have the gumption. And ten years later, they had him declared dead. It's all very suspicious.'

'How dare you.'

Neither of us had noticed Alison coming into the room. 'How dare you, Mother. You promised never to mention that story again. Are you trying to ruin our business?'

'Ruin your business? What about you, ruining my holiday? Using me as unpaid help. I told you; don't borrow money; stick to sheep.'

Alison shouts back. I creep upstairs and put my headphones on. It feels like old times again.

Elsie went off to Bath three weeks ago and has not returned. Alison now has me serving ice-creams in between accompanying tours; it's hard to find time for the toilet, let alone for a lunchbreak. Without our cook, the meals are not nearly as good. I don't complain; I need the job.

As I plod behind the tours, I ponder Edwin's story. Was he present that day? Could he still be down there in the depths? Did his family have him murdered or is it just village tittle-tattle?

Sometimes I think that there are advantages in not having a family.

© Kathy English, 2024

Tidewater

Harry Goode

'…let's not produce darkness at noon, so to speak, by looking at the sun direct.' – Plato "The Laws", *Book X*, translated by Trevor J. Saunders

By the time he was 48, Tom was convinced that he had a purpose of universal significance and that, in due course, it would be revealed to him. It was not that he was of a religious cast of mind. He thought little about such matters. The epiphany that Tom expected had more to do with the nature of existence, that a pattern would somehow become clear.

His life had chugged along by shuffles and chances, and on the whole, he had enjoyed it. However, although his days were full of the usual invented purposes arising from the pressures of work and raising a family, these directions appeared to have no staying power. They came, were fulfilled – or occasionally not – and went their way. Looking back, he could not always recall what had shaped his decisions. In fact, he felt at times he had begun to read events backwards. For example, had he arranged the second date with his wife-to-be, Fiona, in order to pick up Mark, their youngest son, from piano lessons on Tuesday evenings?

One morning in early June he lay awake next to a soundly sleeping Fiona. According to the clock radio, it was 4.34 a.m. but he knew that the light filtering round the curtain edges would prevent further sleep. He started to think of all the times in his life when he had seemed to hover on the brink of ineffable knowledge. They were like the precise moment just before one of those puzzle-pictures resolves itself from being random coloured dots into a hidden scene. The necessary skill he felt to be somewhat similar, to gaze with a look that was simultaneously intent and unfocused. The truth, when it came, would surprise him from the periphery of his consciousness. If he turned his head too soon, it would flit away. He must learn to anticipate without expectation. He was sure that it would not elude him forever.

He carefully shifted his position in the bed. If Fiona stirred, she would automatically turn and lie against him. That would disturb his train of thought.

He recalled how, early one September morning, he had been walking the dog. They had ambled down a quiet, hedge-lined lane. The dog was snuffling in the undergrowth. Tom was thinking about a problem at work. Looking up, he saw that the sun, emerging from behind a hill, was shedding a yellow light into the scarlet-laden branches of a rowan tree. From the top bough, a thrush commenced its repetitive carillon, its phrases spaced and timed with great precision. He stood perfectly still, waiting for the next trilled sequence, which he knew would be charged with an almost unbearable significance. He held his breath.

The dog barked. The bird gave a shrill call of alarm and flustered away.

Once, at a rather boring party, he had suddenly become aware of a dark-haired woman, standing at some distance from him. She was being spoken to by a man who was standing close to her. She was probably listening to him and was looking down. All he could see of her eyes were their pale lids and heavy lashes. At first, he thought that he was simply attracted to her but, of a sudden, he knew that if he could catch her expression when she eventually glanced up, it would reveal the missing pattern, the reason why she and he and everything else had all the weight of existence. He held his breath.

'Be a sweetie,' said Fiona, 'fill my glass for me.'

The table with the drinks was at the other end of the room. When he returned, the woman seemed to have left.

He glanced at the clock – 4.37 a.m.. He thought of another summer's day when the children were young. They had been holidaying on the Welsh coast and had gone to the beach. A heat wave was in progress and, as often happens during such spells, a cool sea fret was still enveloping the beach at mid-morning. With jumpers on, they had organised games on the flat sand to keep warm. A breeze began to disperse the mist and the warmth of the sun could be felt in the gaps before another swirl of moisture closed in. He went to sit on some rocks at a little distance from his family, the better to observe this interesting weather phenomenon. To the right of the cove, cliffs ran towards a headland that was intermittently visible through the haze. Then he knew that when the sun was shining fully on this point, something would emerge from behind it, some visitation, which might have an outwardly normal surface, as a bird or a boat, but which would be freighted with an overwhelming revelation. He held his breath.

'Dad!' said his daughter Jenny, whom he had not noticed approaching. 'Can we have some money for ice creams?'

At 4.39 a.m., he slipped quietly from the bed, gathered his clothes and went to shower and dress in the bathroom. He made a flask of strong black coffee, took a packet of biscuits and some Mahler CDs, left a note for Fiona to the effect that he had gone in to work early and at 5.21 a.m., set out in his car.

It was 10.32 a.m. by his car radio when he turned off the Aberystwyth to Cardigan Road. "*Dunkel ist das Leben, ist der Tod!*" sang the tenor on the CD player. He rounded a bend and there before him was the cove where, so many years before, he had felt the proximity of a great secret.

A line of stubby concrete posts separated the car park from the beach. It was a fine day, with clear, unobscured light. He opened the car door but sat and drank the last of the coffee and ate the last two biscuits before getting out. A middle-aged couple were walking their dog on the sand. It was too early in the summer for families with children to be on holiday.

He crossed to where the cliffs of crumbling, unstable shale began their progress towards the headland, low at first and broken by falls of earth and scree, to which scrub clung precariously, then rising gradually to steeper faces. A footpath was signposted along their base. A notice was affixed: '*Sections of this path are liable to inundation and are dangerous. Check local tide tables before proceeding.*'

He had no expectation that anything of particular

moment lay in the direction of the headland. He could see from the absence of wet sand that the tide had turned and was coming in, but he judged that it would be some time before it came to the base of the cliff. He decided to go some way along the path.

The sun was warm on his back, but a cool air was moving inland off the water and made the effort seem easier. At first, the path rose and fell, following collapsed fractures in the shale, descending briefly and then rising again. Finally, as the cliffs grew taller, it settled to weave among flat rocks at the base. At some point, an attempt had been made at way-marking, white paint splashed on large boulders that had fallen from higher up. Limpets had encrusted and darkened these markings, showing that the high tide must reach this far.

He came to a large rock pool, fully twenty yards in extent, dotted with islands of bladderwrack. He sat at the pool edge, took off his shoes and socks and put his feet in the water. At times the breeze created a *chiaroscuro* of ruffled surfaces. At times, there was stillness, and he could see a pattern of alternating sandy drifts and rocks covered with dark-red sea anemones. Translucent shrimps darted across the sandy stretches, made visible only by their movement. A hermit crab scuttled out from under an overhanging curtain of filamentous weed, bearing its borrowed shell-home as though it were a medieval lady's wimple.

A shrill piping call made him look up. A trio of oystercatchers were making their rapid undulating flight from the direction of the cove. They disappeared beyond the looming headland. Incoming water must have driven them from where they had been feeding.

Raucous gull calls made him look up again. Two birds were engaged in a mid-flight squabble. One had an object in his beak. The other dived at it and the object suddenly fell, landing with a crack on a nearby rock. He walked over to it. The gulls, now united in their outrage at his presence, dived and circled noisily. Lying on its back, broken and oozing, was a crab. One of its claws was missing. The other limbs moved feebly.

He had a sudden sense of the immense cruelty of the beach, its daily drying and drenching, its osmotic excesses, the bludgeon of the waves. No doubt the couple strolling with the dog on the stretched-out sand thought it was a peaceful place. They did not see it was a zone of death, where gulls and oyster catchers tore soft creatures from their crafted caves. The very sands and silts consisted of bones, the shards of defeats. These were the bitter margins of the world.

He could hear the remorseless suck and slap of water on rock, alternating with a noise like air drawn in quickly past clenched teeth. He could sense the rhythm, the mesmerising septet, running on forever... forever... *ewig... ewig...*

The sun had moved to shine fully onto the cliff face. Light bounced harshly on the water, making the surface seem a sheet of slowly swelling white; Tom knew that underneath the water would be dark, as black as a night without Moon or stars.

One... forever... two... forever... three... forever... four... forever... five... forever... six...... forever.........

He held his breath.

Trapped by my Passions

Richard Gould

Saturday, 9th October 1859. The day when my fascination for astronomy began.

I remember that day and its life-changing magnitude as if it were yesterday. Eureka! I had found a purpose in life.

A first feeling was one of relief because physical activities, the usual Saturday morning timetable, had been cancelled to enable the whole school to witness the phenomenon.

We were led onto the field and given sheets of card with tiny prickholes to peer through.

'Do not look at the sun directly,' our master ordered.

'Why not, sir, if it is to be dark?' I asked.

'I will not have insolence, de Villiers,' he declared, his firm slap across my ear augmenting his reprimand.

Others around me laughed, taunting me with cries of, 'Stinky swot.' I was used to their torments, these jibes preferrable though to the bullying I would have been suffering on the rugby field that very moment on a normal

Saturday morning.

And then there was a gasp and a hush as our moon began to pass in front of the sun.

'Protection on now,' ordered our master and I lifted the card, pressing it firmly against my nose.

I watched as the moon, initially in the strong daylight glare little more than a small, faint cloud, slowly approach the sun.

For a brief while it was wholly unseen, but as soon as this spherical object touched the edge of the glowing disk, as if by magic, it became densely black. An eerie shadow loomed, the world around us becoming darker and darker until it was as nighttime, though not exactly so because there was a melancholy aura. As I watched this miracle of an eclipse unfold over an hour and more, I remember my heart pounding. I was witnessing the majestic motions of the heavenly bodies that the Lord has given us. I would dedicate my life to learning about the wonders of our atmosphere.

This was during my final term at a preparatory school in Oxford, with Eton to be my destination the following academic year. I dreaded the prospect, having heard stories from my older brothers of what fellow pupils got up to at the expense of the weaker ones. I imagined that it would be far worse than what I was subjected to at this place.

On the day of the eclipse, I had only recently returned to school from the family home, following the Easter break. I was anticipating my suffering over the subsequent weeks – boarding would be hell, the sports field a torture, and lessons a nightmare with masters seemingly happy to witness the bullying I suffered. Nevertheless, all this would be no worse than what I endured at the de Villiers countryside estate. I was the youngest of four boys. Three were accounted for: one would take over the estate, one be given an army officer's commission, and one would become a cleric. What did that leave for me, an anxious boy who had no interest in farming, hunting, literature or the arts, instead an unhealthy fascination with things celestial?

My father disregarded me. I have a disability with one leg a little shorter than the other (this ailment brutally mocked at school) and it was as if he blamed me for my physical condition. My mother was preoccupied with her entertaining; the two brothers keen on her parties being her favourites. Of my three siblings, one brother bullied me, one ignored me and one pitied me. I cannot now say which of these behaviours was the worst at the time; each of these attitudes contemptible. In childhood, there was never a closeness with my siblings and, sadly, this is still the case.

Such misery I endured during my five years at Eton. Moving on to Oxford University I remained a loner, working long hours in laboratories and at the Radcliffe Observatory where the director, Reverend Robert Main, was my one true confidante.

'Take a post at the Royal Observatory in Greenwich,' Main advised me. 'I can arrange a position there.'

He kept his word and this became my first and, to date, only employment.

The posting has brought me a comfortable existence, augmented by a small stipend received from the family estate after Father died. It is here that I met Lillian, a rare female visitor to the Observatory. That was eight years ago. It is Lillian who steered this lonely soul into marriage, but it has not been a happy one.

I accept I am to blame. I pay her little attention, still less since adding new passions to that of science, passions that swamp me in thought and deed.

Ours is the Age of Collecting. For some this is an insatiable quest for material possessions, an obsession with the output of machines. Fortunately, some good citizens are resisting the march of progress and are instead enthused to reach out to the natural world and to maintain our heritage. I count Donald Montague as one such man. He is my closest colleague at the Observatory, a collector of butterflies who spends his weekends journeying with his nets and containers across the length and breadth of our great land. His display trays are filled with specimens, their bright wings spread open and held in position with tiny brass pins. Another associate, William Southbury, treks over the rough terrain of the Lake District in search of fossils. He has a wonderful assortment and talks about their origins with great zeal. Recently, it was a delight to hear him speak at a Royal Geographical Society meeting in Saville Row. There remains hostility between those for and those against the theories of Charles Darwin, but William dealt with the issue diplomatically, as one would expect from the man.

What are these new passions of mine? One is philately. I am rapidly expanding my collection, aided by the renowned John Edward Gray. I count myself a personal friend of his; indeed, we share patronage of St. James's, rightly considered as one of the more dignified gentleman's clubs in town. It is he who directed me to the shop on The Strand recently opened by Stanley Gibbons where I located a Cape of Good Hope triangular penny brick red. I was able to speak with Gibbons for quite some time, discovering that he intends to pass on ownership of his two shops so that he can concentrate on constructing a record of every stamp produced. This will be a mammoth task.

My wife is uncomprehending of my interest in philately, she calls it my obsession. She will not permit a single stamp to be visible in the house other than those for practical use. Of course I could overrule her, but there are more important matters that require my authority. Indeed, for the sake of safety, it is to my advantage to have a private space away from Lillian, Alice and Mary. Lillian's indifference could so easily cause damage to my collection while she is tidying, and the girls carry the clumsiness of infancy. So I keep my stamps in the attic even though it is a cold place during all but the warmest days of summer and the candlelight is barely adequate.

My collection is housed in a mahogany cabinet, a sanctum of order in a room otherwise filled with hat boxes, glass and chinaware (much of it unwanted wedding presents), and broken heirlooms. There are trunks here, too. They contain fine dresses once worn by a lady keen to be part of the social set, but Lillian's vestments have long since been folded and put away. Sometimes, I open one of the trunks to lift out and hold up an exquisitely embroidered bodice that I keep at the top of the pile. It reminds me of a fleeting moment in time.

As I lean forward on my uncomfortable wing-backed chair without a seat cushion, I hold a magnifying glass in my right hand and the stamp between tweezers in my left. The ½d Russet had appeared perfect, Her Majesty in profile with her hair gathered and folded, but, on closer inspection, I notice a minute rip on the bottom left corner which is a considerable irritation. The value of the stamp is severely lessened by this blemish. I place the stamp on the bare, rough table and take a sip of claret. My concentration is broken and this is not solely by the commencement of Alice's unmelodic thumping on the piano. I have little to do with my children, good-natured though they seem.

Regarding Lillian, I do not treat her unkindly as some men act towards their wives; in return she is civil enough. However, I must declare that civility is insufficient for me. I had hoped for much more from the vibrant, confident young woman who strode into the Observatory and thereafter pampered me with compliments and affection.

I leave my chair and walk to the trunk to retrieve the bodice, a gift from her parents worn on our wedding day. Given what I thought I knew of her – a spirit, a sensualness – her modesty has perplexed me. On our first night together, I was settled on untying that bodice to see her naked. She desisted. I was told to vacate the room while she undressed, that she would call me when in bed. Was this a new bride's shyness, I remember thinking at the time? Alas, it was not. Our short period of intimacy took place in darkness with her passiveness failing to excite me.

It was dear Donald Montague who introduced me to the delights of prostitutes soon after I joined St. James's. The club is a short stroll from where such ladies congregate. Despite the laws of the land, they can be seen openly propositioning gentlemen. I would dismiss my taxi a little distance from the club to walk past the women in the lanes and alleyways only a few steps away from the main thoroughfares.

At first, I shied away from the temptations that these women offered. I come from a devout Evangelist family where such behaviour is most strongly frowned upon. William Gladstone, our Prime Minister, shares similar beliefs and is known for his efforts to rescue prostitutes from the streets of London. And yet, Gladstone apart, there is much hypocrisy regarding this matter. Two of my brothers, claiming to be devout, openly talk of their triumphs, and, at both Eton and Oxford, I saw boys from the most respectful of families flaunt the moral code.

But still this was not for me, despite the growing frustration caused by Lillian failing to meet my physical needs.

One late afternoon, Montague and I were seated in the lounge at St. James's. I must have appeared forlorn despite a cigar in one hand and a glass of excellent port in the other. When he enquired as to the cause of my mood, I blushed and dismissed his question. I would never admit to my domestic turmoil, but somehow he eked out the story of my frustration. In return, he was frank, indeed causing me gross discomfiture, as details of his own transgressions were revealed.

He suggested I join him at Mrs Constable's house, a short walk from St James's. I recall guffawing nervously, pointing out the amusing surname for an illegal house of ill-repute.

'It's safer with a woman from a house and not off the street,' he advised as he topped up my port. I needed the courage provided by drink before agreeing to join him. We staggered through the bustle of West End streets ahead of turning into a darkly lit, unpaved lane.

I was taken aback by Mrs Constable, a toothless, unattractive woman with unhealthily scaling skin. I was close to fleeing if she was to be indicative of the nature of the women who I might encounter. But happily no, for a bevy of ripe young beauties were soon with us, on display to select from.

It took one single night for this pursuit – lying in the arms of a woman willing to satisfy my every whim – to become my second new passion. Philately I can tell all in the world about, but this one must remain my secret and it is a curse. Since that first evening a short while ago, not a week has passed by without several visits to Mrs

Constable.

There is still worse to tell: I have discovered another brothel and am trapped by an addiction that can only bring ruin. With my desires becoming ever more adventurous, some might say perverse, I truly fear for my sanity.

One week ago, I revisited the Stanley Gibbons shop in search of an Indian Dominion first edition missing from my collection. Stepping out on a mild early evening, I decided to walk awhile ahead of catching an omnibus home.

My wandering took me away from the crowds and I found myself amidst a labyrinth of unkempt alleyways. I noted a gentleman seemingly of similar social standing exiting from an impoverished house at the far end of a cul-de-sac and I walked on to investigate.

I knocked and when no one greeted me, pushed the door open. I entered a room with a sweet, cloying vapour that caused me to cough. It was dark, and, before my eyes could adjust, I stepped onto the arm of a man splayed out across the floor. As he growled, I saw others there, men and women in various states of undress.

What a contrast here to Mrs Constable's clean and well-kept place where the women prided themselves in their appearance and would not be out of place strolling along West End's finest avenues in their fancy attire.

The strumpets here were living in a mire of filth. How depraved had I become to want to be part of this? Alas, there was a stirring in my loins followed by an ecstasy spun by the rush of dizziness that the opium brought. These women performed lewd acts beyond anything I had imagined possible.

Enough reminiscing for I cannot remain peering at my stamps any longer tonight; I must go back.

I pour a glass of claret and quickly drink before returning my collection to the cabinet. I extinguish the two candles and leave the attic.

Downstairs I stop at the nursery, returning Alice and Mary's smiles, wishing them well with goodnight kisses. Turning, I see Lillian standing by the doorway.

'I will be visiting the club this evening,' I tell her.

She nods.

'I may well stay overnight.'

Another nod. She is beyond caring.

'Good evening, darling,' I say as I brush past her, planting a kiss on her forehead.

I am trapped in the misery and frenzy of my addiction, utterly ashamed as I step out into the biting cold January darkness to hail a cab.

© Richard Gould, 2024

Twin Lambs

Angela Wray

* 1st place *

'Wrap it round tightly now, Donald. You know what that cold wind on the hill does to your chest.'

Morag fussed over her husband, tying his long scarf round his neck, crossing the ends round under his arms and retying it at the front so that his whole chest was covered with the thick homespun wool. Not even the most vicious nor'easter would be able to penetrate that.

The day had started fine – a sharp frost with a milky pale blue sky and a promise of sun. At this time of year, though, the sun didn't appear over the hill before 11, and by two it was gone. It would be another two months before the cottage felt its warmth again. Morag always loved that day, the day the sun came back. She looked forward to it all winter. When the first beams shone through the little kitchen window and lit up the dust on the flagstones, that was her cue to start the spring-cleaning. That day was a long way off, though; it wasn't even February yet.

The promise of sun hadn't been fulfilled. As the day wore on, upcastings had gathered, a lowering mass of clouds at the far end of the valley away from the sea. Upcastings at this time of year meant snow, and for a shepherd like Donald, snow was the enemy. His ewes were pregnant: losing one of them meant two lives lost, maybe three. First thing that morning, the sheep had been right on the top of the hill, fifteen hundred feet up. If the weather was going to close in, they would have to be brought down to the field by the cottage, to sea level. They would need to be near the byre. Donald would have to give them some of the precious neeps he'd dug a couple of weeks before. Lucky they had – they'd never have got them out now. Morag and wee Eileen had helped him to gather them, lugging them into a great pile next to the byre, ready for this weather.

Morag fetched Donald's long woollen cloak from its hook beside the fire and fussed round him, helping him on with his great boots that had been warming on the hearth.

'It'll be dark before I'm home,' warned Donald. 'I'll take the lamp.' He turned to his daughter. 'Now, Eileen, you be a good girl for your mammy.' He swept the child up and nuzzled her with his great rough beard. She threw her head back, chortling with delight.

'There'll be scones ready when you get back,' Morag said. 'We'll make them together, my lamb, won't we?'

Wee Eileen nodded as her father put her back down. He took up the lamp and went out, his dog at his heels.

They were used to this island life; it suited them. Donald had never known any other: his father and grandfather had been shepherds before him, on the same hill. They had lived in this very house. It was a good warm house in the winter. The big fire saw to that.

Morag's family lived in the village that skirted the shore, half an hour's walk away. She loved the island, tiny as it was. When she was younger, she had walked the whole length of it. A three-day walk. Her mother told her she was mad, but Morag had needed to see it. That was the furthest she had ever travelled. Even though the men in her family were fishermen, Morag had never set foot in a boat. It was considered too chancy: something terrible would happen if you let a woman in your boat. People didn't leave the island unless starvation drove them off. There was everything you could want here.

Morag kept her daughter busy cutting out scones. She tried to stop herself looking out of the window as the flat, unearthly light of the gathering snowstorm enveloped the valley. She built up the fire to cook the scones, then, by its light, she spun and Eileen sewed; though not yet seven, the little girl was making her first sampler. Her mother was pleased – the child was trying hard to get it right, now that she knew all her letters and numbers. They had the minister to thank for that.

The white flakes swirled about the house and sent the wind screaming down the chimney. Morag looked up from her spindle as the door latch rattled, but no-one came in.

Eileen's bedtime drew near, and still there was no sign of her father. Morag followed her upstairs to the tiny room where she slept, in a box bed that was only just long enough for the small six-year-old. This was as long as the bed could ever be, built as it was into the long side of the room. Morag couldn't even stand up in there. It wasn't really a room at all, more of a cupboard built into the eaves, but Eileen loved it.

'It's my room and I have all my friends in here with me.'

Morag always smiled when the child said this; there was hardly room in there for her to kiss her little girl goodnight, let alone fit any friends in. Perhaps she was talking about the mice who lived in the thatch, or the deer who came down from the hill as soon as it was dark and grazed just outside her window.

Morag looked out of the window now, towards the hill. All she saw was a blank white wall that told her nothing, but at least the wind had gone. There was complete silence in the blanket of snow, not even the hooting of an owl to show a sign of life beyond their cottage. What she wanted to hear was Donald's familiar whistle as he called his dog, the alarmed bleating of the sheep as the dog followed his master's bidding and drove them down to safety. She wanted to see the light of Donald's lamp bobbing its way down to the cottage. But there was nothing. Still, at least the storm had blown itself out. She bent down to the child.

'Goodnight, wee lamb,' she said, as she kissed Eileen on the forehead, stroking the mass of russet curls that tumbled about the pillow. The little girl smiled in her half-asleep dream.

Morag closed the door of the little room and went downstairs.

The moaning of the wind in the chimney woke her with a start. She had been asleep in the chair by the fire, but for how long? Where was Donald? Then she remembered. The wind battered at the windows. The byre outside creaked and groaned as if desperate to escape. The storm was back.

Morag wrapped herself up in her shawl just as she had wrapped Donald in his scarf a few hours before, then put on her thick cloak and pulled up the hood. She lit the lamp from the fire, took up her crook and went out into the fierce night.

*

'Mummy, when you come up, can you bring Snowdrop?'
Rachel was only just six, but her voice, coming loud and
clear from the little bedroom upstairs in the holiday
cottage, already had a commanding edge to it.

'Please!' Her mother called up as a sort of reflex action.

'Please!' Rachel echoed.

'Okay. Five minutes. Make sure you're in bed. I'll bring
you a hot water bottle too; it's chilly up there tonight.'

'No, don't. I'm fine!'

Rachel busied herself arranging her menagerie of
teddy bears in the bed. Then, leaving a space for
Snowdrop, she wriggled down under the covers and
closed her eyes.

'Goodnight, wee lamb,' she heard. The soft voice
made Rachel feel warm and comfortable. This lovely cosy
little room with its tiny bed, the gentle kiss on the
forehead, the hand stroking her hair.

'Night, night, Mummy.'

'I'd better go up and say goodnight to Rachel,' said her
mother, putting down her book. 'She'll never go to sleep
without Snowdrop. Hope she'll be warm enough without
a bottle. You never know what the weather's going to do
in these holiday places, especially during the night.'

'She'll be fine,' said her husband. 'You worry too
much.'

Rachel's mother picked up the small white teddy bear
and went upstairs.

The door of the little room was open. She went in.
Through the window there was a sliver of moon, and she
could just make out the figure of a deer grazing on the hill.
There was no sound. What a beautiful, peaceful place, she
thought. I'm so glad we decided to spend Christmas here,
away from the bustle of so-called civilisation.

'Night night, sweetie pie,' she said, tucking Snowdrop under the covers as she bent down to kiss her daughter. The little girl smiled in her half-asleep dream.

Thank you for your purchase!

Did you enjoy Darkness?

We'd love it if you left us a review on Amazon.

Simply scan the code below to leave a review or rating.

Printed in Great Britain
by Amazon